# Moonlight Over Mistletoe

---

Janet Koops

Brown House Books

Book Cover by: The Cover Collection

1st edition 2024

ISBN [print]: 978-1-963745-05-4
ISBN [large print]: 978-1-963745-06-1
ISBN [ebook]: 978-1-963745-04-7

# Books by Janet Koops

## Romance

Magic In Mistletoe
Snowflake Sugar
Moonlight in Mistletoe

## Women's Fiction

Homing Instinct
Six Weeks With You
Rules of Disengagement
Family Friends
Then I Met You

For a complete list of titles, please visit
https://janetkoops.com.

# 1

S TANDING AT THE STREET corner waiting to cross, Eleanor Frost turned her face up to the sun, enjoying the bright warmth after a few days of rain. The winters were long and dark in her corner of Alaska, so she never let the fleeting moments of sunshine pass without taking a moment to enjoy them. Not that it was winter yet, but soon. The days were getting notably shorter.

She crossed into the town square and shook her head at the large Christmas tree that dominated the center of town all year. It was bad enough that the town was named Mistletoe, but about fifteen months ago, it had become permanently Christmas-themed. As it was October, she had to look at a tree adorned with pumpkins and bats wearing tiny Santa hats.

Goodness knew what November would bring. A tree covered with turkeys?

*Carl would have loved it.* She stopped abruptly, facing the tree, and shook the thought out of her head. Focusing on the past was a waste of time. But it was too late. Carl danced in her mind. Oh, how he loved Christmas. The decorations, the parties, the—

"You seem lost in thought."

The words jolted Eleanor out of her reverie. She turned, slightly unsteady from being wrenched from her thoughts, her sharp tongue ready to lash out. But a kind smile and the apologetic eyes of Vivian, her long-time friend, greeted her.

"I'm so sorry if I startled you, Eleanor," Vivian said.

"It's fine," Eleanor said more briskly than she'd intended. "I was merely staring at this tree covered in pumpkins. Have you ever seen such a sight?" A brisk wind caused Eleanor to pull her scarf more tightly around her neck.

Vivian linked her arm through Eleanor's. "Come now. Let's get into the cafe. Hot tea and a crackling fire will do us both some good."

Eleanor nodded, and they walked across the town square to The Cozy Caribou Cafe. While this place didn't tie itself to a Christmas theme like so many other businesses in town, The Cozy Caribou Cafe, or simply 'The Caribou' to locals, didn't shy away from the Alaskan stereotype.

Still, Eleanor couldn't help but feel welcomed by the cafe's log cabin-style rustic exterior and the glow of Edison lights in the window. Once inside, the notes of cinnamon, nutmeg, and pumpkin spice enveloped them. And, while Eleanor couldn't understand the current obsession with pumpkin spice everything this time of year, she found the aroma quite pleasant.

Two years ago, this cafe served its purpose, a relic of past decor and adequate food, but since the renovation and its unapologetic nod to Alaska, The Caribou had become a destination for locals and tourists alike. Rough-hewn timber covered the walls upon which the owners had hung vintage dog-sled equipment, old snowshoes, and large wildlife photographs by a local photographer. But in the center of it all stood Eleanor's favorite new addition: a large, circular fireplace. It crackled and flickered and never ceased to improve her mood, something she needed after allowing thoughts of Carl to enter her mind.

"Look, our favorite table is opening up," Vivian said, tilting her head towards a couple rising from two comfortable leather armchairs on the far side of the fireplace.

"Tourists," Eleanor scoffed, noting the couple's ugly Christmas sweaters.

"Now, Eleanor, be nice. We all know that the upswing in tourism saved Mistletoe," Vivian gently chastised.

"I know, I know. Sometimes it's a bit much, though." She felt Vivian squeeze her arm before they took their seats.

Eleanor removed her scarf and hat and sank down into the soft leather. Vivian followed suit, shocking Eleanor when she removed her hat.

She tried to find words, but her mouth hung open. Finally, she managed, "Viv, your hair."

"What do you think?" Vivian asked.

"I'm literally speechless." Eleanor stared at her friend. Vivian had had long hair since they'd met. Of course, it had been brown then and not the white it was now, but other than the natural evolution in color, Vivian had never, ever changed her hairstyle. Not even one time. It always hung to her waist, pin straight and parted in the middle. Now, it was a pixie cut. A *pixie cut!* But it framed her face beautifully by golly, allowing her stunning blue eyes to sparkle. "You look amazing. You really do."

"Why, thank you. I'm still getting used to it, of course. It feels so strange to wash my hair. It's like there's nothing there. And seeing my reflection in the mirror is still quite the shock."

"What made you do it?" Eleanor asked, still stunned by the transformation.

Vivian linked her fingers together and leaned across the table. "Honestly, something had to change. I've been stuck in a rut. Not that I've been unhappy, but I wouldn't describe myself as happy either. It's been the same thing day in and day out for years. My creative energy has waned, and I just kept waiting for a spark to come along and fire it up again. Then, as I looked in the mirror one day, I said, *Vivian, change will not happen unless you make it so.* And well, here we are."

"Wow. But Viv, you never told me you were feeling so unsettled."

Vivian shrugged. "Honestly, El, I didn't really know how to express it. But now, I feel re-energized. I've got some new sweater designs percolating in my mind, and I love this haircut. It's so darn easy, except that I'll be spending a lot more money at the hairdressers than I used to, that's for sure." She sat back in her chair. "You know me, I'm not a big fan of change, but I realized that opening up to something new might be what I needed. I don't know. After all, it's only hair."

Eleanor nodded. Yes, it was only hair, but Vivian's hair was her signature look, part of her identity. How did one make such a bold decision? Especially at their age. Eleanor wasn't sure she had the courage to do such a thing herself, but she would certainly support her best friend. "Well, to celebrate, coffee and pastry are on me. Your usual order, or are you trying something new too?"

Vivian laughed. "One step at a time, El. One step at a time."

Eleanor stood and walked over to the counter. Behind her, she could hear the gasps of the local townsfolk as they took in Vivian's new look. She set her purse on the polished pine live-edge counter. Max, the Caribou's owner, approached her. It was Wednesday, which meant it was red-flannel day, and Max didn't disappoint.

"What can I do for you, Eleanor? The usual for you and Vivian?"

"Of course," she said.

"That's quite the transformation for Vivian, isn't it?" Max said as he retrieved two peppermint tea bags and dropped them into mugs.

"It is."

"And pretty brave of her, don't you think? I guess it's never too late to change."

Eleanor nodded. "Wait," she called out as Max turned to walk away. "Instead of a bear claw, I think I'll try a slice of the apple pie."

# 2

CHRISTOPHER KRINGLE EASED BACK in his old creaky chair, placing his feet up on his desk. He released a long sigh, then closed his eyes. A quick nap wouldn't hurt. After all, the Zoom call with his grandkids had gone well. Everyone was working hard, and the workshops were chugging along on schedule. With Christmas less than three months away, it paid to stay on top of things.

"Sleeping on the job again, Dad?"

Christoper bolted upright. Shelly, his daughter, stood in the doorway, hands on hips and an amused look in her eyes. "You caught me," Christopher admitted, chuckling. "What can I do for you?"

Shelly entered the office and perched on the corner of his desk after removing a stack of papers and setting them on the floor. "Well, since you asked, you could clean your office."

Christoper rolled his eyes. "Now, Shelly, you know that in spite of its appearance, my office is organized. At least to me."

"It's more like a shrine to Christmas past," Shelly countered, picking up a snow globe and shaking it. She gave Christopher a small smile, her face growing serious. "I'm worried about you, Dad. You really ought to think about retiring. There's more to life than work, you know."

More to life than work? His life was his work. "And let you swoop in and steal my job as head Santa?" he deflected with a joke, wagging his finger at her. "Not a chance. Besides, what would I do with myself? Play shuffleboard in Boca?"

"You don't think I could do the job?" Shelly countered.

"Of course, you could do it. Both you and your brother are more than capable."

"So what's stopping you, then? You could travel and visit your grandkids for something other than work. You could discover a new hobby."

Christoper stroked his white beard. A life beyond Santa duties? What would that even look like? What would he do with all his time alone? Golf? Sure, he enjoyed a game now and then, but he needed to keep busy. No, he couldn't picture it, waking up every morning with nothing to do. The thought terrified him. "This is what I was born to do."

"It's what we were all born to do."

She was right. Was it fair to hang on when his son or daughter could take over? They were both more than competent. In fact, he had no doubt they'd excel. "I know. But I'm not ready to hang up my Santa hat yet. There's still plenty of Christmas spirit left in this old sleigh, you know."

"I know, and I'm not trying to push you out or make you feel like you can't do it anymore. I simply think that you deserve to go out and have some fun. There's a big world out there. Don't you want to discover it?"

Christopher shuffled papers on his desk. The world beyond. That was something he'd not thought about since his Meridith... He shook his head, remembering her smile and the playful glint in her eyes. He closed his eyes momentarily as the ache of loss washed over him. There were some things Christmas magic couldn't fix.

As if reading his mind, Shelly reached across the desk and took his hand. "I know you miss Mom, but filling the void with work is unhealthy. She wouldn't want that."

Christopher nodded. Meridith would want him to retire and hand the reins over to his children.

"She would want you to find something that sparks a new passion."

He gave Shelly a slow nod. "Yes, yes. I know. I tell you what. I'll think about it after Christmas."

"You've been saying that for years."

"Well, this time, I mean it."

"You've been saying that for years, too."

Christopher glared at her over the top of his glasses.

Shelly held her hands up in surrender. "Okay, okay, but how about we make a deal? You try at least one new thing between now and Christmas, and I promise I won't mention retirement again until the new year."

"The lead-up to Christmas is not a good time. You know that."

"I'm well aware. But you'll always find an excuse. Besides, this will let Adam and I take on more responsibility before it's time for us to retire. Let us prove we are ready to fill your big black boots."

Christopher had to admit he wasn't being fair to either of his children. Perhaps the time had come for him to pass on the reins. However, he wasn't sure which one to choose. That was a decision he hoped would work itself out. With a groan, he stood and walked across the room, stepping over piles of paper and around antique furniture. He needed to clean his office before he injured himself. "Coffee?" he asked his daughter as he filled his mug.

"No, thanks."

He rested against the bureau and took a sip. "I'll think about it. That's all I can promise. Just don't go planning your coronation as Chief Operating Santa quite yet."

Shelly chuckled. "I wouldn't dream of it. Besides, I don't look good in red. Adam, on the other hand—"

"Glad to see that you've worked it all out without me," he said with feigned annoyance. At least that Christmas wish came true.

Shelly left his office after giving him a peck on the cheek, and he returned to his desk, nearly tripping over the binder of this year's candy order. He really needed to stop using paper. It's not that he was a technophobe. Far from it, but he liked to see things, to hold them in his hands. Perhaps that's why his office was jam-packed, full of both work and memorabilia.

He picked the glass paperweight off his desk and stared into it as if it would provide answers. The paperweight had been his grandfather's. The desk had been handed down through the generations. The globe had belonged to his mother. Shelly was right in her assessment of his office. It was indeed a shrine to Christmas past. For the first time, Christopher wondered if his grip on the past was so strong that he'd sacrificed his future.

# 3

ELEANOR CLUTCHED HER PARCELS as she exited the post office. The day was spectacular. No wind and not a cloud in the sky. The sun, low on the horizon, was bright and intense, forcing Eleanor to bow her head as tears pricked her eyes. Head down, she didn't notice the solid figure in her path until she collided with what hit like a wall. Her parcels fell to the ground.

Indignation flared. What a careless oaf. Couldn't they see she had her arms full? She snapped her head up, a sharp retort ready on her lips, and froze.

Why, it was Christoper Kringle, Martin's grandfather. He was a large, burly man, probably close to six feet tall. His white hair and white beard certainly played into his name. Still, with a moniker like Christopher Kringle,

Eleanor supposed it was easier to go with the image than fight it. But really, what had his parents been thinking?

She shouldn't have been too surprised to find Christopher in Mistletoe. From what she'd heard, he frequently visited Martin's toy factory. However, the only time they'd met was at Martin's wedding to Sadie, when he'd asked her to dance.

She glanced up to find Christopher's sparkling blue eyes and his white beard twitching with a smile of recognition. Eleanor's stomach dropped.

"Hello, Mr. Kringle. I didn't expect to see you here in Mistletoe."

"Please, call me Christopher," he said as he bent down to pick up her packages. As he rose, packages in hand, and passed them to her, he said, "That was quite the welcome."

Eleanor felt heat creep up her neck, prickling beneath her tightly coiled bun. "My apologies. The sun. It's very bright, you see. Now, if you'll excuse me." She made to step around him, but he placed a large hand on her arm. Oh boy. That touch brought back the memories of his hands when they'd danced. One on her back, the other holding hers, as they'd waltzed. It had been her first dance in years and had felt almost magical. Not that he needed to know that.

"No need to rush off. Tell me how you've been," Christopher asked.

"How I've been?" she blurted out. Immediately regretting it. It was a simple question between two people who'd met before. But aside from Vivian, she'd become accustomed to people being more than happy for her to rush off. Eleanor knew she had few friends. She was fine with that. But was she so out of practice with common niceties that she behaved like a fool? "I'm fine, thank you. Yourself?"

He gave a hearty chuckle. "This time of year keeps me busy."

Was that a hint that he wanted to get going? "Well, I'm sure you have more important business to attend to than standing in the cold with me. I wouldn't want to keep you."

A gust of wind whipped around them, causing Eleanor to shiver and pull her coat tighter.

"Perhaps we could continue this conversation somewhere warmer?" he asked.

What? No. Absolutely not. What would the townspeople think? Eleanor Frost, out socializing with Christopher Kringle. It was ridiculous. "I'm afraid I have errands to run."

"Ah, of course. Another time then, Eleanor."

The use of her first name sent an unexpected jolt through her body.

His eyes crinkled at the corners, and his smile grew beneath his snowy white beard as he stepped back and tipped his hat at her. "It was lovely to see you, Eleanor. Perhaps we'll bump into each other again soon."

Eleanor's step faltered. "Yes. Perhaps," she said, leaving Christopher in front of the post office. She quickened her already brisk pace. What nonsense. He was merely being polite. Yet the memory of their dancing at Martin's wedding surged before her yet again—his steady hand at her waist, the surprising grace in his movements as they waltzed across the dance floor.

Nonsense, she chided herself. Still... as the wind stung her cheeks, Eleanor hoped, just a little, that they might cross paths again.

As Christopher continued down the street, he couldn't help but steal a glance back at Eleanor Frost. Her posture was rigid and unyielding, her sharp features etched with lines of experience and maybe a hint of sorrow. And yet, when they'd danced, she'd transformed. Her movements had become graceful. Her eyes filled with fire.

This stern, prickly woman had him intrigued. He'd known plenty of souls in his long life, but Eleanor's complexity fascinated him.

As he continued along the sidewalk, he noted the crisp fall air, scented with wood smoke and what he believed to be apple pie wafting from the nearby coffee shop. A glorious day for a stroll. Perhaps one day Eleanor could join him? He shook his head, bewildered by his own thoughts. What had possessed him to suggest seeing her again?

"You're playing with fire, old man," he muttered to himself but couldn't entirely suppress his smile.

4

E LEANOR PUSHED THROUGH THE heavy double doors of the elementary school auditorium, her eyes scanning the crowded room. Spotting Vivian's pixie-cut hair peeking above the sea of heads, she wove through the rows of chairs. Vivian waved enthusiastically, patting the empty seat beside her.

As Eleanor made her way through the throng, she swatted at a spider dangling above her seat. "My goodness, would you look at this place? I don't understand why the meeting is here instead of the town hall," she grumbled. Sliding into the seat, she leaned over to Vivian. "Look, the chairs lined along the wall are tiny kid's chairs. They're going to break under adult weight. "

Vivian laughed and shook her head. "You know the mayor. He makes everything dramatic. Perhaps he's announcing a donation to the school."

Eleanor shrugged. "It better be something like that. I swear if Mayor Evergreen called us all here to announce the annual pumpkin pie baking contest again—"

Her musings were cut short as Mayor Gregory Evergreen strode onto the stage wearing an orange suit, black shirt, and orange tie. He stepped up to the microphone and gave it a few taps. The room fell silent.

"Citizens of Mistletoe," he began, his deep baritone echoing off the walls. "Thank you for joining me here tonight. As you've all noticed, our meeting is here in the gym and not at the town hall."

"No, really?" Eleanor whispered sarcastically, resulting in a playful poke in the arm from Vivian.

"Well, there's a dire reason for the venue relocation," the mayor said. "I'm afraid I have some distressing news. After a routine inspection, it's come to light that our beloved town hall is suffering from severe structural issues."

A wave of shock rippled through the crowd. Eleanor sat up straighter, her brow furrowing. The town hall was the very heart of Mistletoe. It hosted every celebration, from the Christmas Eve potluck to the Valentine's Day dance. She'd celebrated her wedding there. The thought of it crumbling broke her heart.

Mayor Evergreen continued, his face grim. "I know this comes as a shock. The town hall has stood for over a century, a symbol of our community's strength and unity. But time and the Alaskan weather both take their toll on even the sturdiest of structures."

Eleanor pictured the grand wooden beams, the creaky old floors, and the historical photographs that lined the hallway. Could it really be beyond repair? What would become of their traditions, their history? Her memories?

Caleb Winters, owner of the general store, shot his hand up. "Mayor Evergreen, what exactly is wrong with the town hall? Surely it's fixable."

The mayor sighed heavily, his torso sagging beneath his festive suit jacket. "I'm afraid the issues are extensive. The foundation is crumbling, the roof is leaking, and the electrical wiring is a fire hazard. Repairing it would cost nearly as much as building a new structure altogether."

Another voice piped up, this one belonging to old Mr. Jameson, the town barber. "But the town hall is a piece of Mistletoe's history! We can't tear it down and replace it with some soulless, modern building."

A chorus of agreement rose from the crowd, and Eleanor nodded along. The town hall was more than just a building; it symbolized their community's spirit, a reminder of all the memories they'd shared within its walls.

But then, a younger voice spoke up from the back of the room. "With all due respect, Mr. Jameson, a new building could be just what Mistletoe needs. Think of the possibilities. We could have a state-of-the-art sound system, energy-efficient heating, maybe even a community gym."

The room erupted into a flurry of chatter as people debated the merits of preservation versus progress. Eleanor chewed her lip, torn between her love of the old town hall and the allure of a fresh start. She'd always vocalized her concern over Mistletoe's old infrastructure, so shouldn't she be on board with a new building? But it was the town hall—anything but that.

Mayor Evergreen held up his hands, calling for silence. "Clearly, this is a decision that affects us all. I propose we put it to a vote. All those in favor of repairing the town hall, raise your hands."

A sea of hands shot up, including Eleanor's and Vivian's. The mayor counted quickly, then nodded. "And those in favor of building a new structure?"

A smattering of hands rose, mostly belonging to the younger crowd. But most of Mistletoe's citizens were loyal to their beloved town hall.

"Well, that settles it," Mayor Evergreen said, relief in his voice. "We'll begin fundraising efforts immediately to cover the cost of repairs. It won't be easy, but if there's one thing I know about this town, it's that we always come together when it matters most. So with that in mind, we need your help. If anyone has any ideas for fundraising events or initiatives, please don't hesitate to share them. We're open to all suggestions."

The room fell silent, the weight of the challenge settling over the crowd. Eleanor's mind raced, searching for a solution. Suddenly, an idea sparked to life. Did it stem from the memory of her and Carl dancing on the town hall grounds at their wedding reception or the more recent dance with Christopher? She wasn't sure. All she knew was that a plan was quickly forming in her mind.

She moved closer to Vivian, her voice low so that only Vivian would hear her. "What about a ballroom dancing competition? We could hold it in the town square, charge an entry fee, find sponsors, and offer prizes for the winners. It would be a fun way to bring everyone together and raise money at the same time."

Vivian's face lit up, and she nodded enthusiastically. "Eleanor, that's brilliant. You should suggest it to the mayor."

But as quickly as the idea had come, Eleanor's confidence faltered. She glanced around the room, taking in the faces around them. The thought of standing up and speaking in front of everyone made her palms sweat and her heart race. She knew she was regarded as the town cynic. People might reject her idea because she herself was always so critical.

"I can't do it," she said to Vivian, shrinking back in her seat. "It's a silly idea."

Vivian tapped Eleanor's leg reassuringly, then stood. "Mayor Evergreen, if I may?"

The mayor nodded.

"I think having a suggestion box where people could submit their ideas would be helpful. That way, everyone can contribute without feeling put on the spot. It will also give us all a few days to develop sound proposals."

Mayor Evergreen stroked his beard thoughtfully. "An excellent idea, Ms. Miller. We'll set up boxes around town and give everyone a week to submit their suggestions. Then we'll review them and decide on the best course of action."

As the meeting adjourned, Eleanor gave Vivian's hand a grateful squeeze. "Thank you," she whispered.

Vivian smiled. "That's what friends are for, El. Just promise me you'll write up your proposal."

Eleanor hesitated. She didn't want to make a promise that she might not keep, but then she remembered how she and Carl had exchanged vows in the town hall, and Eleanor silently swore she'd do everything she could to save the building that contained so many memories. "I promise."

# 5

ELEANOR SAT AT HER desk, a hot cup of tea steaming beside her. She wiggled her fingers, stretching them out, before placing her hands on the keyboard and typing.

Ballroom Dancing Competition Proposal

She stared at the screen. Blink. Blink. Blink. The cursor pulsed rhythmically, like a digital heartbeat summoning memories of Carl. "Silly woman," she said, yet the ache grew as thoughts of Carl threatened to overwhelm her. How she would give anything to once again brush her lips against his, stare into his dark brown eyes, run her fingers through his thick, wavy hair, and feel the heat from his hand on her back as they glided across a polished dance floor.

But that would never happen. They'd shared their last dance. "You're so beautiful," he'd told her when they'd won the Starlight Swing Competition. He'd squeezed her hand, his shoulders back, so proud. Then he'd collapsed, and all their hopes, dreams, and love had died along with him on the floor that terrible, terrible night.

"I can't do this," Eleanor said, pushing her chair away from her desk. She entered the kitchen, her hands shaking as she filled the kettle for another cup of tea, even though her old one remained untouched. It was something to do, something to occupy her mind. As long as she kept busy, no matter how trivial the task, she could keep her grief at bay.

Still, years and years of suppressed emotions had lodged an enormous ball of anger deep into her heart. It wasn't fair that Carl was taken from her so long ago. How could someone so full of energy, light, and love just die? A brain aneurism, that's how.

A sob escaped her. Time didn't heal her wounded heart. She'd been without Carl for twenty-five years, and yet her grief felt so fresh, so raw. Indulging her melancholy, she pulled out the photo album she kept in the side table drawer, the edges worn from the countless times she'd thumbed through its pages. With a shaky hand, she opened it to a brighter time.

"Oh, Carl," she whispered, tracing his face with a wrinkled finger, "Look at us on the dance floor, we were wonderful, weren't we?" In the photo, Eleanor's younger self beamed, her sequined dress catching the light as Carl held her close. "That was the first competition we won, remember?"

Then she flipped to the next page. She and Carl stood in front of a large studio window. Above them, a sign read: Frost Dance Studio. They were smiling as they cut a ribbon for the grand opening. Nothing could dampen their spirits that day, not even the cold Seattle rain. A tear hit the page, and she quickly wiped it away.

She'd call Vivian and tell her she'd tried to write the proposal but that it was too hard. Vivian would understand.

Eleanor turned another page, and there they were, at the town hall, having said their vows in front of a justice of the peace. Vivian and a small group of their friends were throwing rice over them as they walked out. "I miss you, Carl," Eleanor said, "Every single day."

But staring at the picture gave her strength. Their dance studio was long gone, as was their Seattle apartment, but the town hall? She could hold on to that.

Eleanor stood determinedly, made her cup of tea, and sat back at the computer. She began typing. "This is for you, Carl."

---

Two weeks later, Eleanor found herself back at the school gymnasium. It was hot and stuffy as she waded through the aisle, wedging between Mildred King, the librarian, and Vivian.

"My word," Mildred said, "I haven't seen this many people in one place since last year's chili cook-off disaster."

Eleanor sniffed. "Well, let's hope this gathering doesn't end with the fire department being called." Vivian let out a small laugh and gave Eleanor a friendly pat on the arm. "Eleanor, be nice."

Eleanor nodded at her friend, but she had been trying to be funny.

She turned in her seat, glancing around the gym. She caught Stanley Boone's eye behind her. He moved forward in his seat, smelling of cheap cologne. "What do you think, Eleanor? I bet there's been a bunch of wacky ideas."

Eleanor bristled, her spine stiffening. "Did you propose anything?"

"Well, no."

"Then don't be so quick to judge, Stanley."

Not waiting for Stanley's reaction, Eleanor turned back to face the front. She knew he'd be shocked, as typically they mocked people together.

Luckily, Mayor Evergreen took to the stage, ending any further chance of conversation.

"Here we go," whispered Vivian.

Eleanor smiled and nodded despite thinking she might be sick. She'd poured her heart into that proposal, but what if the mayor's office hated it? What if she became the laughingstock of Mistletoe? She was about to get up to leave when the mayor began speaking.

"Good evening, everyone. Wow! Look at this turnout. What a town we have, eh? What a town!" The mayor took a moment to look across the crowd. "Now, let's get down to business, shall we?"

The audience applauded.

"So, after a week of studying all the fundraising ideas, we have selected three to help us reach our goal of renovating the town hall." He took a sip of water. "The first is a crowdfunding option submitted by Matt Leclerc, our local tech wiz. I think this will be quite successful, especially if we can tap into the pockets of all the tourists who have graced our quaint town since becoming a Christmas-themed destination. Thank you, Matt, for your proposal."

Cheers and applause came from the crowd.

"Next, we have a silent auction, and believe me, this isn't a small affair. Already, there are companies willing to make significant donations. The Mistletoe Inn and Spa have donated a couples weekend. Northern Bound Expeditions has donated two trips. One is a northern lights viewing weekend, and the other is a dog sled camping trip. Those are only a few of the local companies willing to make a difference. So a big thanks to Marshall and Ilene Hendrix for their idea and hard work at finding sponsors before the proposal was even accepted."

Again, the audience clapped and cheered.

Eleanor relaxed. There was no way her idea was being chosen.

"And now, our third and final selection, something a little different, and something I think will liven up the long fall nights, a ballroom dancing competition!"

Eleanor's jaw dropped to the floor. Surely, she'd misheard.

"This proposal caught our attention because of its fun nature. It's something we can all participate in, and the person who submitted this believes that with her connections, we can have professional dancers compete as well. If it turns out half as good as the proposal, we are in for a treat, ladies and gentlemen, a real treat."

"But I can't dance," someone cried out.

"Then you should learn," the mayor responded. "I'm sure there are dozens of YouTube videos out there."

The crowd murmured in agreement.

"Who came up with such an idea?" someone shouted.

Eleanor's momentary elation was quickly replaced by panic. She hunched her shoulders, trying to make herself as small as possible. But a voice inside her, one that sounded suspiciously like Carl's, said, "Stand up, Ellie. It's your time to shine."

With trembling hands, Eleanor slowly rose to her feet. "I did," she said.

The gymnasium fell silent. All eyes turned to Eleanor, looks of disbelief etched on their faces. Eleanor felt her cheeks burning. "I used to teach ballroom dancing," she explained. "With my late husband, Carl."

Beside her, Vivian began clapping, and then everyone joined in.

Eleanor's heart raced, but not with fear. In fact, there arose a feeling she hadn't felt in years: determination.

But as Eleanor walked home that night, and the initial rush faded, a new worry crept in. "What have I gotten myself into?" she wondered aloud, her mind racing with potential disasters. It could be awful... or it could be marvelous, a little voice said. And for the first time in a long time, Eleanor chose to believe in the latter.

# 6

T HE AROMA OF CHEESE and tomato sauce wafted through Christopher's kitchen as he carefully pulled a bubbling lasagna from the oven. Setting it on the counter, he wiped his brow with his hand. "Ho, ho, you're looking mighty fine," he murmured to the dish. This was Meridith's recipe, and he'd done her proud.

Christopher glanced at the clock. The grandkids were to arrive soon. Each fall, he made dinner for his grandkids, most of whom were regional Santas, but there were also others who played equally critical, though less public-facing, roles. Tonight, he was hosting Martin, the Santa for the West Coast, along with his daughter Nora and one of Shelly's sons, Jack, who lived in the same town as Martin.

Jack had struggled to find his place in the world, and, much to Christopher's surprise, he'd found it working at the Snowflake Sugar Shop in Mistletoe. While Jack was loved by his family, he'd always felt out of place because his magic wasn't Santa magic. Instead, he could manipulate snow, ice, and frost, but his true talent lay in chocolate. Christopher couldn't imagine a life outside of the Kringle family business, but Jack was incredibly happy.

Right on time, the doorbell chimed, pulling him from his thoughts. He swung the door open. "Welcome, welcome."

Nora wrapped him in a hug. "It smells awesome in here," she said. "Let's eat. I'm starving."

"Well now, dear Nora, let me take your coats before we sit at the table. There's plenty to go around," Christopher chuckled.

Jack playfully elbowed Martin. "Tell me, cousin, why you can't use your Santa magic to cook like this?"

Martin laughed. "Because then you'd be over at my house more than you already are."

"Now boys," Christoper said, "This was your grandmother's recipe, and the secret ingredient is love, not magic."

Nora rolled her eyes. "Really, Great-grandpa? That's so cheesy. Can we just eat, please?"

They all laughed, and Nora, Jack, and Martin settled around the dining table while Christopher fetched the steaming lasagna and set it in the center of the table. "Nora, please bring out the garlic bread and salad."

"You bet," Nora said and returned quickly, carrying both items, a piece of garlic bread hanging out of her mouth.

"Well, thank you all for coming," Christopher said. "Let's dig in, and then you can tell me what's going on in Mistletoe and how the Christmas preparations are going."

Martin took a hearty bite of lasagna and grinned. "Grandpa, this is delicious. You've outdone yourself."

Jack nodded in agreement, then leaned forward, and Christopher noted the mischievous glint in his eye. "You know, with skills like these, you should consider opening a restaurant. It'd be a great hobby."

"You've been talking to your mother, evidently," Christopher said, taking a sip of wine. So this was where the conversation was going.

"Don't you think it's time for a little fun outside of work?" Martin asked.

"It's a bit late now, boys. I'm too set in my ways," Christopher said, hoping to end the conversation.

"Well, if Eleanor Frost can change, you certainly can," Nora said. "She's organizing a ballroom dancing competition for the town hall fundraiser."

Jack nearly choked on a bite of garlic bread. "Eleanor Frost? As in our resident Grinch?"

"Come now, Jack. Don't be so harsh," Christopher gently reprimanded.

"Grandpa, you don't know Eleanor," Jack said.

"But he does," said Nora. "They met at Dad's wedding. They danced the night away."

Heat blossomed in Christopher's cheeks. "Nora, my dear, we did not dance the night away. We shared a waltz."

"Still," Nora insisted, "you two were great together. You floated across the floor." She clasped her hands together, held them against her heart, and fluttered her eyelids. "It was so romantic."

Jack burst out laughing, causing Christoper to take a long sip of wine. "And what's so funny?"

"You... and Eleanor... dancing," Jack sputtered. He started coughing, and Martin had to slap him on the back. "Easy there, I bruise like a peach," Jack said to Martin.

"Okay, so while I don't share my cousin's level of shock," Martin began, "I, too, find it an unlikely fit."

"Let's set the record straight," Christopher said. "First of all, we danced at your wedding. I did not propose marriage. Second, I enjoyed our dance together. And lastly, need I remind you not to judge someone until you've walked a mile in their shoes? We are Kringles. I expect better."

"Yes, Grandpa. Sorry," Jack said, yet his expression remained playfully defiant. It was the same look Jack had as a boy when he'd 'accidentally' turned Christopher's toilet into ice.

"What's that look for?" Jack asked.

"I was remembering the time you froze my toilet," Christopher said.

"You did what?" asked Nora.

"A story for another time, and believe me, it's a good one," Jack told her. "As for now, I'd like to hear more about Eleanor's ballroom dancing contest. Rosie and I were away when they announced the winning proposals."

Martin turned to Christopher. "The town hall needs some desperate renovations. They were looking for ideas."

"And Eleanor's ballroom dance contest was one of three proposals to win." Nora took a bite of lasagna. "Oh." She covered her mouth with her hand and swallowed. "I just got the best idea, ever."

Christopher raised an eyebrow. "And what is that?"

"You sign up for the contest."

The room fell quiet. "Me?" Christopher asked.

"Why not? You like dancing. It's a good cause and need I remind you, we're Kringles. It's our duty to spread goodwill and cheer."

"Nora," Martin warned. "Don't get cheeky."

"I'm not. I'm serious," Nora said. "Mistletoe needs participants and Great-grandpa can dance. We have to save the town hall, Dad, we have to."

"She raises a good point," Jack said. "And it will get my mother off your back about finding a hobby."

Martin nodded.

Christopher considered it. One night to get Shelly off his back? "When is this event?"

"I don't think the date has been announced yet, but my guess is that it will be before Christmas. The mayor wants things to happen fast. The crowdfunding page went up the day after he announced the winning proposals," Martin said.

"That makes the decision for me. You know this is our busiest time of the year. I can't neglect my Santa duties."

"It's not a huge commitment," Jack said. "Plus, have you ever heard of the word *delegate*? You have an army of people working for you."

Christopher glared over his glasses at Jack. "Yourself included. Don't forget that." The thing was, his grandsons were right. It was not a huge commitment at all. One night of dancing to have Shelly off his back. That was a risk worth taking. "Alright," he told them. "I'll do it." He held up his wineglass. "Here's to the ballroom dancing contest."

# 7

E LEANOR TOOK A DEEP breath and squared her shoulders as she pushed open the glass door of the library's meeting room. As she stepped inside, five pairs of eyes turned to greet her, curiosity and skepticism evident in their expressions.

"There she is. The woman of the hour," said Mildred King, the eternally chipper head librarian. Eleanor fought the urge to roll her eyes at the woman's saccharine tone.

"Hello," Eleanor said and took a seat at the long table. She scanned the faces around her, mentally cataloging their potential reactions to her proposal.

Caleb Winters, the general store owner, offered a kind smile that she pointedly ignored. The man was nice to everyone. Then there was

Sadie Kringle, the Miami transplant who'd taken over the Snowflake Sugar Shop and married Martin. Of course, Mayor Evergreen's overly perky assistant, Gloria Woodward, gave her a wide, practiced smile without even a hint of sincerity.

Bert Jones, the bank manager, spoke up. "Shall we begin? Eleanor, I believe you have a presentation for us regarding the ballroom dance fundraiser?"

Eleanor nodded stiffly, her fingers tightening around the folder in her lap. "Yes. Of course. I've prepared a detailed outline of the event." She stood, hoping no one would notice her shaking hands as she distributed copies of her meticulously crafted plan. The room silenced, save for the sound of flipping pages as each committee member read it through. Eleanor sat back in her chair and braced herself for the inevitable criticism and judgment.

"This is quite comprehensive," Caleb remarked. "I'm impressed, Eleanor."

Surprise flickered across Eleanor's face before she could school her features. "Well, I'm glad you think so," she said. "I don't do things by halves."

As the committee members began to nod and murmur appreciatively, a flicker of confidence ignited within her. She launched into the proposal's details.

"What about judges?" Bert inquired, leaning forward with interest. "You've mentioned judges but have included no names. Do we have qualified individuals in town?"

Eleanor's eyes glinted. "As a matter of fact, I've contacted several former colleagues from my competitive dancing days and asked if they'd be interested in serving as judges." Sending those emails out had been one of the hardest things she'd ever done. It had been years since she'd contacted any of them, and she'd expected either a curt no or no reply at all. But much to her surprise, everyone had been so gracious and happy to hear from her. "It's hard for anyone to commit as we don't yet have a date, but I've already had interest from several of them."

A hush fell over the room. Caleb's eyebrows shot up. "Competitive dancing? Eleanor, I had no idea you had that kind of background. I knew you had once owned a dance school in Seattle, but I didn't know that you danced, at least not at that level."

Eleanor lifted her chin, a whisper of pride creeping into her voice. "Yes, well, there's a lot you don't know about me, Caleb. My husband, Carl, and I were champion ballroom dancers."

"That's incredible," Gloria breathed, genuine admiration in her eyes. "Your expertise will be invaluable in making this event a success."

Eleanor straightened her posture. "Yes. I hope it will. Now, let's discuss the finer points, shall we?"

As the meeting progressed, Eleanor became fully immersed in the planning process, her usual negativity temporarily forgotten in the face of her rekindled enthusiasm for dance.

Near the end of their allotted hour, Gloria tapped her pen against her notepad, her eyes bright. "I think I've found the perfect date. How does the weekend after Thanksgiving sound to everyone?"

A chorus of agreement rippled through the room. Sadie clapped her hands together, her voice brimming with enthusiasm. "Oh, that's great! It's our busiest time of year. There will be so many tourists here. We need to think of ways to get them involved. What about fan favorites? And we should have it in the town square. That way, everyone can watch. I know it will be cold, but we'll put up a large tent with heaters. I'm sure the staff at Martin's workshop can help us."

Eleanor scowled. "That's all well and good, and I like your venue suggestion, but the date Gloria is proposing is only six weeks away," she said. "It's an awfully tight timeline."

Bert furiously wrote notes on his handout, his usually cautious demeanor replaced by uncharacteristic optimism. "But think of the potential. We could kickstart the holiday season with a bang. And let's be frank about this, people make a lot of donations during this time of year. We can't waste the opportunity."

Caleb nodded vigorously. "I agree. It's ambitious, but I believe we can pull it off."

Eleanor pressed her lips into a thin line, weighing their enthusiasm against her natural inclination towards pessimism, or in this case, reality. After a moment, she let out a resigned sigh. "Very well. If you're all committed to making this work, I suppose I can't object."

"Excellent!" Gloria exclaimed, already scribbling furiously in her notepad. "Now, expect an email from me later in the week with a list of actionable items."

The committee members agreed and packed up their items, ready to leave. Eleanor stood, gathering her papers. The nervous energy accompanying her into the meeting had transformed into determination. As she made her way to the door, she couldn't help but feel exhilarated.

The crisp Alaskan night greeted her with moonlight shining over the town square. It was beautiful and graceful. "That's it", she said aloud. "Moonlight Over Mistletoe." It was the perfect name for the ballroom dance competition. She'd email the committee as soon as she returned home.

She practically skipped down the street. It had been a long time since she'd felt a sense of purpose and a connection to the passion that had once defined her life.

# 8

THE CARIBOU'S WARMTH ENVELOPED Eleanor as she scrutinized the papers spread before her, lips pursed in concentration. Across the table, Vivian sipped her latte, serving as a sounding board for Eleanor's ideas.

"So, we've got confirmations from three professional couples already," Eleanor said, tapping a nail against the list. "And sponsorship from the Snowflake Sugar Shop and Caleb's General Store. But they're also on the committee, so I expected it."

"Don't look a gift horse in the mouth, El. The competition will be here before we know it."

"Don't I know it? Will the people who want to participate have time to learn and practice? I bet half the people in The Caribou right now probably think the foxtrot is some kind of animal track."

Vivian let out a snort. "Oh, El, you're so funny."

Before Eleanor could respond, the cafe's bell chimed, and Eleanor turned towards it. Her breath caught as Christopher Kringle's imposing figure stood in the doorway, his white beard gleaming in the light, his cheeks rosy from the cold, and his smile so large, his eyes crinkled at the corners.

Why did he always have to look so jolly?

Christopher's eyes swept the cafe, landing on their table. Eleanor's stomach knotted as he approached. Why on earth was he heading towards them?

"Well, hello there, ladies. Eleanor, Caleb told me he saw you coming over here. Mind if I join you?"

Before Eleanor could protest, Vivian chirped, "Of course not. Please, sit down. I'm Vivian, by the way."

"Yes. Of course. I remember you from Martin's wedding." Christopher settled into the chair, his presence somehow making their cozy corner feel smaller. Eleanor busied herself shuffling papers, determined not to meet his gaze.

"Actually, Eleanor, there's a reason I was looking for you," Christopher said, his voice as smooth as honey. "I heard about your ballroom dancing competition and want to sign up."

Eleanor's head jerked up. "You what?"

Christopher's eyes crinkled with mirth. "Is that so hard to believe? I may be no Fred Astaire, but I can cut a rug with the best of them. I think I held my own when we danced."

Flustered, Eleanor wiped imaginary crumbs off her lap. "Well, yes. Of course." She became acutely aware of Vivian's poorly concealed smile.

"I... well... I suppose..." Eleanor stammered. "If you're sure you want to participate."

"Absolutely. So, where do I sign up?"

"You can sign up online or at Caleb's store."

"Don't you have some extra copies of the signup form, El? I thought I just saw some," Vivian said.

Eleanor shot her look. "Well, yes. I think I do."

As she fumbled for the registration form, Vivian stood abruptly, her chair scraping against the floor. "I think I'll grab another coffee. Eleanor, Christopher, can I get you anything?"

"No, thank you," Christopher replied. Eleanor shook her head.

Vivian sauntered away, leaving Eleanor alone with Christopher, his jovial presence filling the space between them.

"So, Eleanor," Christopher leaned in, "what sparked you to organize a ballroom dancing competition? I'd love to hear more about it."

Eleanor's fingers tightened around her mug. "I'm a dancer. Or I was. It's been a long time," she muttered, fixated on the swirling coffee. "Carl, my late husband, and I used to compete professionally. We also owned a studio in Seattle."

"Really? That's fascinating. What was your specialty?"

A ghost of a smile tugged at Eleanor's lips. "The Viennese Waltz. Carl always said I floated across the floor like a snowflake."

"I bet you were magnificent," Christopher said.

"We were a good team, my husband and I," Eleanor said, her gaze growing distant as she drifted back in time. She could almost feel the satin of her favorite gown and hear the music swelling around her. Blinking, she forced herself back to the present. "It was another life," she said. "Before I left Seattle, before I lost Carl, before everything changed." Eleanor cringed. She'd said too much. What was wrong with her?

Christopher's large hand covered hers, startling Eleanor. "I understand. Losing a spouse, it leaves a hole nothing can quite fill."

Eleanor's eyes snapped to his, finding genuine empathy.

"I think that's part of the reason my family has been pushing me so hard to try new things recently. My wife has been gone for a long time, and I know it's time to retire, but the thought of doing it alone..." Christopher's voice trailed off. "They worry, but sometimes you simply want to wallow in peace," he finished, chuckling.

Despite herself, a smile tugged at her lips. "I've become quite proficient at wallowing." Their eyes held, a silent understanding passing between them, putting her at ease, so much so that she revealed to Christopher what she'd admitted to no one, not even her best friend: "But unbeknownst to Vivian, she's inspired me to step out of my comfort zone." Suddenly, his motive for entering the dance contest dawned on her. "Your family put you up to the ball-room dance competition, didn't they?"

Christoper pulled his hand away. "Well, they suggested it, but I never do something I don't want to. And besides, it's for a good cause."

"It certainly is," Vivian's voice cut in.

Startled, Eleanor turned to see her friend sliding back into her seat, a mischievous grin on her face. Vivian placed a coffee in front of Eleanor and a hot chocolate in front of Christoper. "I know you both said no, but I couldn't resist."

"Thank you," Christopher said. "One of my favorites."

"Yes. I thought you were a hot chocolate kind of guy. So, are you signed up yet?" Vivian asked him.

"No, not yet."

"Well?" Vivian glared at Eleanor. "What are you waiting for? Give him the form."

Eleanor reached into her folder, pulled out a registration form, and then passed him a pen.

Christopher donned a pair of reading glasses and quickly completed it. "I put Martin's address as my own. It's easier that way."

"I guess it's hard when your address is simply The North Pole," Vivian said, and Eleanor kicked her under the table. Fortunately, Christopher laughed.

"As you can imagine, I get that a lot," he said.

"Yes. I should think so," Eleanor said, taking the paperwork and sliding it back into her folder. She already had several completed forms, having picked them up from Caleb's store. So why did this one feel more... significant?

# 9

T HE FIRST SNOWFALL OF the season had dropped two inches of snow on the streets of Mistletoe. Eleanor, snug in her new boots, couldn't help but admire how pretty the town was under a blanket of white.

Just as she was passing the general store, Caleb came out, a friendly smile lighting up his face. "Eleanor, I've been hoping to catch you."

"You have more registrations for me?" she asked.

"Yes, but that wasn't why I wanted to talk to you." A gust of wind caused Caleb to shiver. "I was wondering if you'd consider teaching some dance lessons. A bunch of us have gotten together to practice what we watched online, but to say it was a disaster is putting it mildly."

Eleanor's lips pursed into a thin line. "That was a lifetime ago. I haven't taught in years." *Nor have I taught without Carl. How could I do it alone?*

"Please consider it. We could use the high school gym. I already cleared it with Principal Smythe. She said the gym is empty on Tuesday and Thursday evenings and that she might join in. I also thought we could offer a prize for the beginner group. Best new dancer, or something like that."

"That's not a bad idea," Eleanor said. Caleb certainly had put some thought into all of this. Her resolve wavered. "Fine. One class to start, and we'll see how it goes. Next Tuesday, at 7pm, in the gym. Don't be late."

"Thank you, Eleanor," he said, leaning down and quickly planting a kiss on her cheek. "You won't regret this." Caleb then turned and crossed the street.

"I hope not," she muttered, stunned by both her agreement and by the appreciative kiss.

<hr>

The following Tuesday, Eleanor pushed open the heavy gymnasium doors, her dance shoes tucked under one arm. The sight that greeted her stopped her in her tracks.

More than two dozen eager faces turned towards her, the room buzzing with excited chatter. Adults, young and old, and even a few teenagers packed the space, all waiting expectantly.

Eleanor's stomach churned. She'd expected two, maybe three people.

She scanned the crowd, searching for Caleb's familiar face. When she found him, her eyes narrowed.

He shrugged, a sheepish grin on his face. "Word got out. Turns out a lot of people want to learn."

Eleanor closed her eyes and inhaled the familiar scent of polished wood floors. Instantly, old memories stirred—Carl's laughter, the swish of skirts, the thrill of perfecting a difficult step.

*I can do this,* she thought, standing tall. *For Carl. And maybe for the person I used to be.*

With newfound determination, Eleanor strode to the center of the room, her stern expression sweeping over the assembled crowd. "All right, everyone. Let's start with the basics."

The group quietened and circled Eleanor. She became so nervous she wondered if she could even speak. But she had to do this. So, taking a sip from her water bottle, she began.

"Since we don't have much time, we will have a crash course on the basics. Now, we're going to review the most important elements of ballroom dancing. First, let's focus on posture. With posture comes grace and poise. Without it, you might as well be stumbling around like a drunken moose."

She demonstrated, drawing herself up to her full height, chin lifted. "Your spine should be straight, shoulders back. Think of a string pulling you up from the top of your head. See what I'm doing, copy me."

Everyone did their best to copy her posture. "Excellent," she said. "Another fundamental aspect of ballroom dancing is that it is based on structured and standardized movements. The dancers follow specific steps and patterns."

Eleanor moved across the floor in a box step, her footwork precise and measured. "Experienced dancers add their own flair to the movements, but the dance steps are always the same."

The crowd's eyes followed her movements, curiosity and apprehension on their faces. Eleanor suppressed an eye roll. This was going to be a long night.

"The last key point I need you to remember is the connection to your partner. You need to work in harmony. This comes with practice, trust, and communication." *And chemistry,* she thought. She and Carl had plenty of that. "Based on our limited timeframe, I think it best that we have three lessons, and you learn a new dance at each one. Tonight, we will cover the waltz. Next time, the foxtrot and lastly, the rumba."

"I watched a couple on TV do the Argentine Tango. Can we learn that?" a teenage girl with blue hair asked.

"Ah yes, that is quite the dance, passionate and intense, and a bit beyond the beginner's skill level. Let's start with these three and see how it goes."

The girl nodded.

"All right. We'll start with the basic box step."

Once they practiced the step individually, Eleanor used Caleb to demonstrate how to hold your partner. After which, Eleanor directed them to partner up. As the participants scrambled to pair up, her attention zeroed in on a young couple. The man's hand resting awkwardly on his partner's waist. Eleanor slid it up to the woman's shoulder blade.

"Remember, this isn't a barn dance," she said to the entire room, not wanting to embarrass the couple. "Proper frame, please." Eleanor moved through the crowd, adjusting postures and repositioning hands. With each correction, she felt a familiar spark ignite within her.

"Eleanor, why do we need to keep our elbows up?" a middle-aged woman asked, her brow furrowed in concentration.

"It's proper form and will take some getting used to. Imagine you're balancing a cup of hot cocoa on your elbow. You wouldn't want to spill it all over your beautiful dress, would you?"

A ripple of laughter spread through the gymnasium.

Another hand shot up. "How do we know which foot to start with? I forget."

"For heaven's sake," Eleanor muttered under her breath. Louder, she said, "Gentlemen, you always start with your left foot. Ladies, your right foot. Now, everyone, take a deep breath, and we'll take our first step."

As she surveyed the room, Eleanor's eyes landed on Caleb, who was attempting to lead his partner. His face was a mask of determination, but his movements were stiff and awkward. Despite herself, Eleanor felt a twinge of something. Fondness, perhaps?

She smiled. "All right, everyone, let's try it with music," she said, striding over to the ancient record player she'd dropped off earlier in the day.

As the strains of a waltz filled the air, Eleanor watched the couples move. It was far from graceful, but as time passed, there was a marked improvement from the beginning of the class. She allowed herself a small nod of satisfaction.

*They were not entirely terrible*, she thought as the music faded.

Several beaming faces turned towards her. "Eleanor, that was so much fun. Will you be teaching more classes? I mean, after the ballroom dance competition, so that we can get better?" a young woman gushed, her eyes sparkling enthusiastically.

Eleanor blinked, taken aback by the earnest request. "Well, I hadn't really considered it. Perhaps," she said slowly, her mind already spinning with potential lesson plans.

As the participants filed out of the gymnasium, chattering excitedly about the upcoming dance competition, Eleanor lingered. She ran a hand over the smooth surface of the record player, but surprisingly, she wasn't lost in memories. She was thinking about the future.

# 10

CHRISTOPHER STOMPED THE SNOW off his boots as he and Nora entered Martin's cabin.

"Dad, we're home," Nora called out.

Martin came to greet them at the door. "And how is your Aunt Jamie, Nora?"

"She's good. Her birthday party was awesome. It's too bad you couldn't make it. Oh, and the cake Rosie and Jack made was incredible."

"Good, well, hopefully I can make it next year."

"Yes, that would be great," Christopher said. "Other than on Zoom calls, I can't remember when all my grandchildren were together at once."

"We are spread all over the world," Martin reminded him.

"Yes, yes, I know. But it's not like you're flying economy. Santa magic makes travel much easier, does it not?"

Martin rolled his eyes. "Well, come on in for a drink before you head home. I just made some tea."

Christopher nodded and removed his boots and coat. Martin's cabin was always so cozy. He dropped onto the worn leather sofa, hoping he wouldn't fall asleep. It had been a long day.

Martin soon joined him in the family room, handing him a steaming cup of tea.

"I was at the general store today, and you should have heard Caleb. All he could do was talk about Eleanor's dance lesson. Apparently, she taught a group the waltz last night," Martin said with a chuckle. "I never would have guessed that Eleanor would have the patience to teach, but Caleb said she was terrific."

Christopher nodded. Eleanor had already revealed her past experience to him at The Cozy Caribou. "If I have learned anything, it's that humans are complex and multifaceted. Sadly, we often judge them too quickly."

Nora plopped down into the armchair, and Christopher noted the devilish flicker in her eyes. "Why don't you ask for a lesson, Great-grandpa? I know you can dance, but how often do you do it? I'm sure a refresher lesson or two couldn't hurt." She waggled her eyebrows. "A private lesson or two, that is."

"Nora," Martin chastised. "Be respectful."

"I am," Nora protested. "I'm just trying to move things along. I think Great-grandpa likes her, so why waste time?"

"Nora," Martin repeated, and this time she held her hands up in surrender. "Okay, okay."

Christopher was grateful for his beard, as he was certain his whiskers would hide the blush on his cheeks. He thought of dancing with Eleanor, as they had at the wedding, and honestly, he quite liked the idea. Oh dear, was his blush deepening?

He placed his teacup on the coffee table and stood. "Well, thanks for tea, but I must be going."

Martin made to stand.

"Don't get up," Christopher said. "I'll see myself out." Several minutes later, he stood on

Martin's porch, his heart pounding with both exhilaration and nervousness, steeling himself for what he was about to do.

He called to his horses, and before he could change his mind, he was winding his way through the Mistletoe streets toward Eleanor's house. Soon, he was standing on her porch, knocking on her door.

Eleanor answered immediately, her eyes widening at the sight of him. "Christopher? What on earth are you doing here?"

He felt like a nervous teenager. Clearing his throat, he spoke. "Good evening, Eleanor. I heard you were providing dance lessons. And while I already know how to dance, I thought, maybe, you could give me a refresher lesson, privately, if possible." He cringed inwardly at his awkwardness, imagining the look Nora would give him as he stumbled through each word.

Eleanor's brow furrowed. "I'm a little busy organizing the competition," she said matter-of-factly.

Christopher nodded. "Of course, my apologies for disturbing you." But then he noticed a flicker of something, he wasn't sure what, pass over Eleanor's face.

"But a little practice with a suitable partner would be good for me, too." She gave him a small smile. "Would tomorrow at noon work for you? I know it's soon, but I have so much to do and—"

"Tomorrow at noon would work fine," he interrupted. "I know the perfect place, quiet and out of the way. I'll pick you up then."

Christopher turned and rushed back to his sleigh, fearing an awkward silence would fall between them if he remained on her stoop. He gave her a wave and took off into the night. He knew precisely where and what he wanted to do for tomorrow. Now, he just needed to work a little magic.

<hr>

At noon the next day, Christopher guided his horse-drawn sleigh to a stop in front of Eleanor's house.

He saw the curtains draw back and her face peer out the window. Seconds later, she emerged from her home, her eyes fixated on the carriage. "What is with you Kringles, and your love of sleighs? I would think a 4x4 or a snowmobile would be far more practical."

Christopher chuckled as he extended his hand to assist her into the sleigh. "All I can say is that we are traditionalists." He climbed in after her, taking his seat at the reins. They set off, and he attempted to make small talk. "Beautiful day, isn't it?"

"Hmm," Eleanor responded. "Where exactly are we going?"

"You'll see."

"That sounds ominous," Eleanor said.

Again, Christopher laughed. "Not at all. It's a place my grandson Jack told me about. It's a little out of the way but quite beautiful and secluded."

Eleanor gave him an odd look. "Are you embarrassed to be seen with me? The gossip works its way through Mistletoe quite quickly."

"Oh no, nothing like that," Christopher said, finding her bluntness both surprising and refreshing. "Heck no. It's somewhere peaceful where we can dance to our heart's content without interruptions."

"If you say so," Eleanor said.

Finally, they pulled up to the clearing, and Christopher heard Eleanor gasp. As a Santa, he was accustomed to gift-giving and providing joy in the Christmas season, but it was, in many ways, an anonymous gift, and, more often than not, he never witnessed gratitude directly.

But here he was, bringing a small pleasure to a person he knew and who he'd like to believe was becoming a friend. Hearing that little catch in Eleanor's breath as they reached their destination was incredibly rewarding.

"I've lived in Mistletoe most of my life," Eleanor said, her eyes taking in the clearing, the treeline, the crisp blue sky. "How have I never stumbled upon this place before?"

Christopher chuckled softly. "Sometimes the most magic is hidden in plain sight," he said, squeezing her hand. "We just need the right moment to discover it."

Eleanor turned to him. "Well then, we better not waste it. Let's get dancing."

They walked down to a frozen lake. "It's not slippery?" Eleanor asked.

"I should think not. Black ice is the slipperiest and best for skating. There is too much wind at this lake to make black ice, and with the recent snow, the surface is rough."

"You're quite the expert."

"Well, part of it comes with experience; the other comes with Google."

That caused Eleanor to smile.

"Shall we?" Christopher asked, offering his hand. "We could start with a waltz. I don't have music, but perhaps you could count the beats?"

Eleanor nodded, slipping her hand into his. They began to dance, and as Christopher heard Eleanor count 1,2, 3–1,2,3, he would have sworn that music emanated from the very trees themselves.

Slowly, Eleanor's rigid posture softened. Christopher marveled at the grace in her movements, the way her feet seemed to float across the lake. As they twirled and swayed, he found himself lost in her eyes, seeing past her stern exterior to the passionate dancer within.

"I'm relieved that my memory of you as a dance partner didn't fail me. You're not half bad," Eleanor admitted, a rare smile tugging at her lips.

Christopher chuckled, allowing a bit more energy and flair to enter his steps.

As they danced across the ice in perfect sync, Christopher sensed a deepening connection between them. Their movements flowed seamlessly, matching the splendor of the crisp winter day. The rhythmic crunch of their steps on the ice and the warmth of the sun on their faces created a shared moment of pure joy. Christopher relished this growing bond, silently hoping Eleanor felt it, too.

They whirled through a tango and a foxtrot, and as they were finishing a rhumba, Christopher noticed that Eleanor's eyes glistened with unshed tears before a single droplet escaped, trailing down her cheek.

"Eleanor?" he prompted, slowing their movement. "What's wrong?"

Eleanor's breath hitched, her controlled demeanor crumbling. "I haven't danced like this since Carl's death. I'm sorry."

Christopher's heart ached at the pain in her voice. "What happened?"

She looked away, but he lifted her chin and stared imploringly into her eyes. "Hey, you can tell me. Or not. Whatever you're comfortable with."

The silence stretched out like a long winter night, and Christopher ached to comfort her. He wrapped his arms around her, pulling her close, content to provide her with nothing more than a shoulder to cry on. But then she spoke.

"We were competing and had won our competition. Carl was laughing, telling me how beautiful I looked, and then he collapsed. Right there on the dance floor." Her voice broke. "Brain aneurysm. He was gone before the ambulance arrived."

"Oh, Eleanor," he whispered, his own memories of loss rising to the surface. "I'm so sorry. While everyone's experience of loss is unique, I understand that pain, that emptiness."

"It was so long ago, and yet...how do you do it? How do you move on?" she asked, her voice muffled against his parka.

"I wish I knew," Christopher said, rubbing soothing circles on her back. "I think that we always carry our lost loves with us. They're a part of us. But I'm also beginning to discover that we need to find happiness in the memories, and not only pain."

"I hope you're right," Eleanor said. "The night he died, I vowed never to dance again. I sold our dance studio, moved back to Mistletoe, and lost contact with all my friends in the dance world. And I never danced until you asked me at Martin's wedding. That one dance began to rekindle a part of me I'd buried along with Carl. I want to remember Carl and me dancing with fondness, and I know Carl would want me to dance. He'd be heartbroken at the angry and bitter woman I've become. So I'm trying. For him. For me. But it's hard. Change is hard."

"Oh, Elenor," he whispered, gently kissing the top of her head.

They stood there, holding each other, sharing a moment of vulnerability and understanding that transcended words.

After a while, Eleanor shivered, so Christopher pulled back. "Come on," he said. "Let's go warm up."

He led Eleanor back to the sleigh, producing a thermos from beneath the seat. "Hot chocolate," he explained, pouring two steaming cups.

"Thank you for today," Eleanor said. "And I'm sorry for my behavior. I don't normally reveal my feelings like that. I'm terribly embarrassed."

"Don't be," he insisted. " I'm glad I was here for you. I'd like to think we're becoming friends."

"Me too," Eleanor said, and they clinked their mugs together.

As they sat side by side, sipping their cocoa, Christopher hesitated momentarily before slowly slipping his free hand into Eleanor's. To his surprise and delight, she didn't pull away.

# 11

E LEANOR'S EYES SCANNED THE program for the umpteenth time, chewing on her lip in concentration. The surrounding kitchen starkly contrasted her intense focus—calming yellow walls adorned with vintage dance posters, the aroma of freshly brewed coffee wafting from an antique percolator.

"Do you see any typos here?" Eleanor asked Vivian, sliding the paper across the table.

Vivian reviewed the document. "It looks fine to me, El. You've checked it a dozen times already."

Eleanor sighed. "I know, but it's the program. We will look like amateurs if there is a mistake. I'm sending it out to some dance organizations and schools. I know it's getting close to the date, but some more dancers might be interested. If there are mistakes, we won't be taken seriously. And we can completely forget about sponsorships."

Vivian nodded, her quiet agreeability a soothing balm to Eleanor's frayed nerves.

"Here's the checklist," Eleanor said. "Let's review it." She took a moment to stretch her back. "The mayor's office is securing the tents for the town square. Mayor Evergreen's niece created a website for ticket sales and registration. The tourism department is distributing promotional material to everyone on its mailing list. The Mistletoe Business Bureau is seeking sponsorships. Caleb is organizing the heating and the special flooring for the dancers. Mistletoe Events is providing the tables and chairs, and the high school promised us some bleachers if necessary, and—" Eleanor was interrupted by the ping of a text.

She glanced at her phone. "Hold on. It's the florist." Her heart sank as she read the text. "Oh, no."

"El, what is it?"

"There was a major power outage in Silverpine Ridge, where the florist is. Their inventory is ruined, and their pipes froze and burst, flooding the store. They won't be up and running by Thanksgiving. What are we going to do?"

Eleanor paced around the room.

"I have an idea," Vivian said.

"What? Tell me." Stress had made Eleanor's eye twitch.

"Instead of real flowers, get the Snowflake Sugar Shop to create the large centerpiece and then smaller edible bouquets for the tables."

"You've got to be joking."

"I'm not. You've seen Rosie's sugar work. It's fantastic."

Vivian was right. Despite Eleanor's grumpy demeanor whenever she entered Snowflake Sugar, she had noticed that Rosie and, yes, even Jack were incredibly talented. Not that she'd ever admitted it.

"I don't know, Viv. That's a lot to ask."

"Didn't you say Sadie was on the committee?"

"Yes, but..."

"But what?"

"It's embarrassing to ask for help. I don't want people to think I made a mistake and they are doing me a favor."

"That's ridiculous. Regardless of why you need it, I'm sure they'll be more than happy to help. So can you please promise me you'll ask them?"

Eleanor hesitated, her jaw tightening from her internal struggle. Finally, she sighed. "Okay. I guess there is no harm in asking."

Vivian stood and wrapped Eleanor in a hug. "Great. Now tell me about the judges you secured."

Excitement rushed through Eleanor, her lips curving into a proud smile. "I called up some old connections. It's been years, but they accepted my invitation." She ticked off names on her fingers. "First, there's Dmitri Volkov, the Russian ballet master. He's as strict as they come, but he knows talent when he sees it. Then there's Lucinda Fairfax," Eleanor said, her voice softening with fondness. "She was my roommate at dance academy. Retired now, but she was a star in her day. And finally, Antonio Moretti, the

Italian ballroom champion. He's still quite the charmer, even in his seventies."

Vivian grinned at her friend. "Eleanor, I must say, you're different. Happier, even. Your voice has a lilt to it I haven't heard in years."

Eleanor's cheeks flushed, caught off guard by the observation. "I don't know about that," she deflected, adjusting her tight bun nervously. "Oh, alright. I suppose organizing this competition has been fulfilling. It's reminded me of my love of dancing, and I'm trying to focus on that instead of the painful memories tied to it because of Carl. There I said it."

"And?" Vivian prodded.

"And, what?"

"What about your growing connection to a certain Mr. Kringle?"

Eleanor remembered his kindness at the dance lesson, the way he'd held her as she poured her heart out. "Perhaps Christopher has something to do with it, too. He's not entirely insufferable."

"That's high praise coming from you," Vivian said, laughing at Eleanor's grudging admission.

"But seriously, it's good to see you passionate about something again. The whole town's noticed how involved you've become."

Eleanor nodded slowly, surprising herself with her next words. "It's been nice, actually. Feeling connected to Mistletoe again. Not just as an observer, but as a participant." She shook her head as if to clear away the sentimentality, yet a smile tugged at her lips. "But don't you go spreading that around, Vivian Miller. I have a reputation to maintain."

"I wouldn't dream of it," Vivian said. "Now, let's make some more coffee and get back to work."

"Yes, but first, I need you to know that I couldn't have done any of this without you," Eleanor said. "Your support has been invaluable."

Vivian reached across the table, patting Eleanor's hand. "That's what friends are for, El. I'm just glad to see you finding happiness again."

A lump formed in her throat from such an open display of affection. She cleared it gruffly. "Yes, well, thank you. I mean it."

They shared a laugh, years of friendship filling the kitchen. Eleanor glanced at the papers strewn across the table. They would finish the planning to finalize the event that afternoon. A sense of accomplishment washed over her.

"We're almost there, Viv," she said, allowing a small smile to grace her lips. "This competition might actually be a success."

Vivian nodded, gathering the papers into neat piles. "It will be. You've poured your heart into it."

Eleanor nodded as a flutter of elation ran through her.

"I honestly believe that Mistletoe's first ballroom dance competition is going to be a night to remember," said Vivian.

"You know, I think you might be right."

# 12

CHRISTOPHER'S EYES TWINKLED AS he settled into his plush, red armchair, the glow of his laptop illuminating his face. His fingers flew across the keyboard, clicking through a myriad of websites showcasing activities in Alaska.

After the pleasant afternoon he'd spent with Eleanor, Christopher wondered if his daughter had been right. Getting away from work proved good for him. Maybe he could semi-retire. The thing was, having someone to do activities with made it much more appealing.

"Ho ho! What do we have here?" he chuckled, leaning closer to the screen. An article about dog sledding caught his attention, the image of majestic huskies racing across a snowy landscape filled him with wonder.

Perhaps, but he didn't know if Eleanor liked dogs. He also imagined her teasing that it was just another kind of sleigh.

He continued to scroll.

Christopher scratched his beard as he read. Ice fishing. Now that was an activity he hadn't tried even after a lifetime of living in the north. He could almost smell the cold, clean air and taste the fresh catch cooked over an open fire.

Yes. Ice fishing would be perfect.

His heart raced with anticipation as he reached for his phone, eager to call Eleanor. But just as his fingers brushed the device, it rang.

"Good afternoon, Christopher here," he answered, his tone welcoming.

The voice on the other end was frantic, detailing a crisis at one of the toy factories.

"Let's not panic," he soothed. "What seems to be the problem?"

As he listened to the details, Christopher's first instinct was to drop everything and rush to the factory. But then Jack's advice entered his mind. *Delegate.* Yes, he needed to delegate more. And why not start today? Then, he could still make plans with Eleanor.

"I understand the urgency," Christopher said firmly. "I'll send Shelly or Adam right away. They can handle this situation."

After a call to Adam, Christopher exhaled, relaxing. He picked up his phone again, this time dialing Eleanor's number. His finger shook slightly.

"Eleanor? It's Christopher. Do you have a minute to chat?"

"Yes. I do."

"Wonderful." He then proceeded to explain his idea.

"Ice fishing?" Eleanor did not sound convinced.

"Now, don't knock it 'til you've tried it," Christopher said. "Picture this: a crisp winter morning, the lake like a sheet of glass. You're bundled up, a thermos of hot cocoa at your side. The anticipation as you drop your line through the ice."

"Sounds cold."

"Ah, but there's more," Christopher said. "Think of the camaraderie, the stories shared. And when you feel that first tug on your line? There's nothing like it."

"I thought you said you've never tried it."

"I haven't, but that's how the website describes it."

Much to his relief, Eleanor laughed. "You know I'm responsible for the dance contest. I can't possibly take time away now."

"Oh, I understand completely. It's my busy season too, what with toy production ramping up. But sometimes a break can do wonders for productivity and creativity."

There was a long pause. "Perhaps."

"Think about it. A little adventure might be what you need to breathe new life into your contest planning."

"Well, I suppose I could give it a try."

"Great." Christopher flipped through his planner. "How about Monday?"

Eleanor agreed, and he hung up the phone before sending out an email informing his staff that he would be unavailable on Monday. Shelly would question him right away, of course. But he'd deal with that when it happened. Right then, he wanted to savor the moment.

# 13

T HE BELL ABOVE THE Snowflake Sugar Shop door jingled merrily as Eleanor stepped inside, her lips pressed into a thin line. The sweet scent of frosting and sugar assaulted her senses. She straightened her spine, steeling herself for the task ahead.

Eleanor's eyes swept across the quaint shop bursting with color, from the rainbow display of glittering candies to the pastel-painted walls with whimsical paintings. Glass jars and metal tins of various sizes lined the shelves, each one packed with sugary treats. The floor was a checkered pattern of white and pink tiles, and a large crystal chandelier hung from the ceiling, casting a warm glow. Combined with the sweet smell of sugar and chocolate, Eleanor's senses were overwhelmed. Was that why she'd always been so rude?

Her attention turned to Sadie and Rosie, organizing a new truffle selection. With measured steps, she approached them, her hands clasped tightly in front of her.

Sadie looked up. "Good morning, Eleanor. What can we do for you?"

"I need your assistance," Eleanor began, the words tasting bitter on her tongue, but she forced herself to continue. "For the upcoming ballroom dance competition. The florist, who was supposed to create our main centerpiece, lives in Silverpine Ridge and—"

"Did they get hit by the power outage?" Rosie interrupted. "I heard half the town is without power."

"Yes, that's correct, and even though it is still two weeks away, they fear they will not be up and running soon enough to provide us with the centerpiece. That's where you two come in."

Sadie's eyebrows shot up in surprise. "Of course, Eleanor. We'd be happy to help."

Rosie's eyes lit up as she nodded enthusiastically. "We'll come up with something fabulous. Don't you worry."

"Perhaps a cascade of sugar snowflakes?" Sadie suggested.

Rosie chimed in, "Or a miniature ice palace with spun sugar icicles!"

Eleanor blinked, taken aback by their eagerness. These women were certainly exuberant.

"We could incorporate edible glitter for extra sparkle," Sadie said.

"And maybe some delicate sugar ribbons in cool blues and silvers," Rosie added.

Eleanor's brow furrowed. "It mustn't be gaudy or overstated."

Sadie nodded solemnly. "Of course not. We'll make sure it's elegant and refined, just like ballroom dancing."

"We promise to work hard and create something perfect for you," Rosie assured her, her smile friendly and genuine.

"Thank you," Eleanor said. "Sadie, I believe you know our budget and have an idea of what the Silverpine florist was supposed to deliver. You should have received the quote in an email two weeks ago."

"I did, and I do, so trust us, Eleanor. Rosie and Jack will deliver something amazing. Our centerpiece will be worthy of the ballroom dance competition."

"Speaking of dancing," Rosie said, "how are things going with Christopher? I heard you two had a dance lesson."

Eleanor's spine stiffened. "I fail to see how that's any of your concern."

"Oh, we didn't mean to pry," Sadie interjected, her tone softening. "We just thought—"

"You thought wrong," Eleanor snapped, her fingers curling into fists at her sides. "My personal affairs are precisely that, personal."

Rosie's smile faltered, but she pressed. "We only asked because—"

"Because what?" Eleanor's voice cracked, betraying her vulnerability. "Because you'd love some gossip about my private life to spread around town?"

The shop fell silent. Eleanor's cheeks burned, realizing how abrasive and defensive she sounded. She closed her eyes briefly, summoning all her inner strength. *Change is hard.* "I apologize. That was uncalled for."

Sadie reached out, her hand hovering near Eleanor's but not quite touching. "It's okay, Eleanor."

Eleanor looked up, surprised by the genuine concern in both women's eyes. There was no judgment, no hidden agenda. Just kindness and understanding.

"Christopher is kind," Eleanor said. "It's been nice, having someone to dance with and talk to."

Rosie's smile returned, friendly and encouraging. "That's lovely."

Nodding curtly, Eleanor made for the exit. "Well, I need to get going. Thank you again for your help with the centerpiece. I have no doubt it will be stunning."

She was filled with a sense of lightness as she left the Snowflake Sugar Shop. The winter air tingled against her cheeks, but she barely noticed. Her mind whirled with emotions—relief about the centerpiece, yes, but something else, too.

She paused, glancing back at the cheerful storefront. Change was hard, but she'd made progress. *One step at a time.* Isn't that what Vivian had said after cutting her hair? Changing her own attitude had shown her that there was more to Sadie and Rosie than she'd initially thought. Maybe there was more to herself.

# 14

ONDAY MORNING, ELEANOR STOOD on the edge of a frozen lake, her breath forming misty clouds. The winter landscape stretched before her, a pristine blanket of white broken only by the dark silhouettes of pine trees. She tugged her scarf tighter, eyeing the expanse of ice with trepidation.

"Beautiful, isn't it?" Christopher's voice broke through her thoughts. He trudged up beside her, pulling a wagon full of fishing gear.

"If you enjoy being surrounded by nothing but cold and quiet."

Christopher chuckled. "Oh, you'll see. There's more to it than that. At least, I hope there is."

Eleanor laughed, slapping him playfully on the arm.

As they ventured onto the ice, Eleanor's steps were hesitant. "Are you certain this is safe?"

"Absolutely. I had Jack check it for me and he's kind of an ice expert." Christopher set down his equipment and began to unpack. "Here, why don't you help me set up the auger?"

Eleanor eyed the device skeptically. "And what, pray tell, is an auger?"

"It's for drilling holes in the ice," Christopher demonstrated. His strong hands guided the tool. "Want to give it a try?"

Reluctantly, she took hold of the auger. Eleanor's gloved hands gripped the handle. The metal blades of the auger bit into the frozen surface with a satisfying crunch. To her surprise, she found a spark of satisfaction in the task. "I suppose it's not entirely unpleasant."

"Such enthusiasm," Christopher teased. With the hole drilled, Christopher set up the pop-up shelter and placed two folding chairs inside it. Also in the wagon were blankets, warmer clothes, and a cooler of snacks.

A smile tugged at Eleanor's lips. "A cooler? Don't you think it's cold enough already?"

"Ah, yes, well. Consider it a warmer. This way, the food won't completely freeze."

Eleanor settled into a folding chair. The inside of the shelter was surprisingly cozy. "You know," she conceded, "this isn't quite as dreadful as I imagined."

"I'm beginning to learn that is high praise coming from you, Eleanor Frost." Christopher gave her a playful wink. "Just wait until we catch something." He baited her hook. "Ready to drop your line?"

Eleanor hesitated, then nodded. An incredible calmness washed over her as the line sank into the icy depths. The shelter was cozy and intimate. Protected from the wind, she was quite comfortable. And Christopher had thought of everything. Thermoses of hot chocolate and soup. Decadent brownies for dessert. Blankets for their laps.

She and Christopher fell into an easy conversation punctuated by comfortable silences. It was as if they were off in their own little world.

"I must say, Christopher," Eleanor mused, "this has been a pleasant surprise. I didn't think—"

Suddenly, her fishing rod jerked. Eleanor's eyes widened. "Oh! Oh my, I think I've got something."

Christopher moved closer. "That's it, Eleanor. Now, start reeling it in, nice and steady."

Eleanor gripped the rod tightly, her knuckles turning white as she struggled against the unseen force beneath the ice. "It's quite strong," she exclaimed, a mixture of exhilaration and frustration coloring her voice.

Christopher moved closer, his face creased with concentration. "You're doing great. Let me help you."

His large hands enveloped hers on the rod, and Eleanor felt a jolt that had nothing to do with the fish. Together, they reeled the fish in, their movements synchronizing as if they'd done this a hundred times before.

"That's it," Christopher encouraged. "We're wearing it down. Just a little more."

Her arms ached, but Eleanor found herself oddly unwilling to give up. "I never thought I'd say this about fishing, but it is rather exhilarating."

Christopher chuckled. "Wait till you see what we've caught. It feels like a big one."

With a final, mighty pull, their prize broke the surface. Water splashed, momentarily obscuring their view. As it cleared, Eleanor gasped. "Good heavens. It's enormous."

A silver-scaled fish thrashed at the end of the line, easily the size of Eleanor's arm. Christopher quickly moved to unhook it, his hands gentle but firm.

"It's a beautiful Arctic Char," he explained, holding it up for her to see. "What do you think? Should we keep it or let it go?"

Eleanor hesitated, torn between pride in their catch and empathy for the creature. "I think we should release it. Let it live to fight another day, as they say."

"I couldn't agree more, but first, let me take your picture with it."

After posing with the fish, she released it back into the water. As they watched the fish disappear back into the icy depths, she turned to Christopher and said, "Perhaps there's more to this ice fishing business than I initially thought."

"That's because you're the one who caught a fish," Christopher laughed.

"That's zero for you, and one Arctic Char for me." Eleanor raised an eyebrow. "Wait a minute. Was that really an Arctic Char? I didn't think you fished. How would you know?"

"I have no idea," Christopher confessed, laughing harder. "That's the first name that came to mind. Sounded correct though, didn't it."

Eleanor's laughter joined his, and soon they were caught in a fit of giggles like two little kids.

As their laughter wound down, Eleanor leaned into Christopher and kissed him on the cheek, hoping it would convey more than her words ever could. "Thank you for convincing me to try something new."

Christopher's smile widened. "Anytime, Eleanor. Anytime."

As they trudged back across the ice, Eleanor couldn't help but wonder what adventure with Christopher might come next.

# 15

"HERE, LISTEN TO THIS," Eleanor said to Vivian. She pressed play on her answering machine.

"Hello, Eleanor, this is Sadie. Don't panic. Everything is fine with the centerpiece. I'm actually calling to invite you over for Thanksgiving dinner. You probably have plans already, but if not, we're having a big dinner here and would love to have you. Okay. Let me know."

"Well, isn't that something," Vivian said.

"What should I do?" asked Eleanor. When Vivian was in town and not spending Thanksgiving in Fairbanks with her daughter, Eleanor usually had dinner there. Otherwise, she would help at the local hospital, making dinner for staff and patients who couldn't spend the holiday with family.

"You should go," Vivian said.

"I'm not sure. What about the hospital?"

Vivian dismissed her concern with a wave. "Help with prep, then head over to the Kringle's' house for dinner."

"You make it sound so easy."

"It can be if you let it."

Eleanor had her doubts.

"Thanksgiving is about community and giving thanks, which is what you do at the hospital, but it's also about friendships, old and new."

"Other than you, I prefer my own company," Eleanor insisted.

"Come on, Eleanor," Vivian said. "You don't prefer it. You've merely created a self-imposed exile. Just look at how much happier you've been since working on the ballroom dance competition and putting yourself out there. And my goodness, El, read between the lines. They're inviting you because Christopher will be there."

"Do you think so?" Eleanor couldn't help but smile at the thought of having dinner with Christopher.

"Absolutely, but even if he's not, go have fun. When was the last time you let yourself enjoy something without reservation?"

"I think it was in the nineties," Eleanor joked, but sadly, it was close to the truth. Or at least it was until recently. Ballroom dancing reminded her of times when joy wasn't a stranger. But also, in the mix, were fresh memories from dancing in the woods and catching a fish with Christopher.

Vivian glared at her, awaiting an answer.

"Fine," she acquiesced. "I'll go."

<hr>

Eleanor stepped onto Sadie and Martin's porch. Hesitation nipped at her resolve, but the soft glow of lights and the rustic nature of the log cabin drew her in. The rich aroma of roasting turkey and pumpkin spice enveloped her senses as she tapped the door knocker twice before it swung open fully.

"Welcome, Eleanor." Sadie greeted her with a smile, pulling her into a hug that was surprisingly nice. The house's interior glowed with amber lights, and garlands of autumn leaves intertwined with twinkling fairy lights ran down the banister and over the fireplace.

"Thank you for having me," Eleanor replied, her voice steadier than she felt as she handed over the bottle of wine she'd brought.

"Come in, come in," Martin boomed from the living room, his grin infectious as he waved her over. "What can I get you to drink? Rosie made mulled wine, and we have soda, water, and beer."

"The mulled wine sounds lovely," Eleanor said, standing in the middle of the room like a fish out of water.

"Come sit by the fire with me," Nora said. Eleanor gave her a smile, grateful to the girl for offering her a seat.

"A girl at school said you're going to teach ballroom dancing at the community center. I've always wanted to learn, so count me in," Nora said.

"That's not exactly what I said. But maybe one day."

Laughing at one of Jack's jokes, Rosie caught Eleanor's eye. Rosie tugged Jack over to join Nora and Eleanor. Jack tipped an imaginary hat in Eleanor's direction. "Glad you could make it, Eleanor," he said.

Eleanor inwardly cringed from all the times she'd been rude to Jack. The man never seemed to take anything seriously, but she'd been wrong. He'd worked tirelessly to help Rosie create a massive moving candy sculpture for Valentine's Day. It was the talk of the town, make that the county. She didn't deserve Jack's kindness, yet there it was.

"I was happy about the invitation," Eleanor admitted, the words no doubt surprising Jack, but he hid it well.

The festive atmosphere was settling into Eleanor's bones when the front door opened, and she heard Christopher's voice, causing her heart to flutter. He entered the room wearing a red sweater, and with his white beard and perfectly Santaesque hair. Eleanor turned to Nora and said, "Please tell me he works as a mall Santa during the holidays. That level of similarity should not be wasted."

Nora grinned, nodding her head. "Something like that."

"Ah! I see I'm the last to arrive. Happy Thanksgiving, everyone." Christopher's booming voice enveloped the room, his positivity infectious.

He hugged his family members and then walked towards Eleanor, who stood. "Happy Thanksgiving, Christopher," she said. Surely, her voice didn't waiver. Did it?

"And to you, I'm happy to see you here." Then he moved forward and brushed her cheek with the lightest of kisses. Yet it had her heart racing and her cheeks flushing.

The Kringle family's banter was light and included the kind of gentle teasing that happens within close-knit families. The conversation included Eleanor. She was asked about Mistletoe in the old days, what it was like before she left for Seattle, and how she found it when she returned. The longer she was there, the more relaxed she became and the more she shared about her past.

When Martin announced that dinner was ready, fate or perhaps a conspiratorial Sadie seated her and Christopher together, their elbows brushing as they settled at the elaborately set table.

"Tell me, Eleanor, do you still follow the ballroom competition circuit?" Martin inquired, his interest genuine as he carved into the turkey.

"Only casually," Eleanor said. "But this ballroom dance competition has rekindled my interest."

"I'm happy to hear it," Christopher said. "There's something almost magical about dance, isn't there?"

"Indeed, there is," Eleanor agreed, "When dancers master the precision of each step, they lay the groundwork for artistry. A couple moving with both technical skill and chemistry can cast a spell on their audience."

As plates were cleared and laughter echoed around them, Eleanor realized the evening had brought forth an unexpected harmony between her old life and the potential for new beginnings. And much of it was thanks to the

man beside her, whose very essence whispered promises of enchantment in the most
ordinary moments.

The clink of cutlery had given way to the
shuffle of feet as the group migrated from
the dining room to the coziness of the living
room, where the fire crackled merrily in the
hearth. Martin rummaged through a wooden
chest and pulled out an assortment of board
games.

"Let's play charades," he declared, and the
suggestion was met with an enthusiastic chorus of approval.

Except for Eleanor. "I don't think so," she
said. "You all play. I can be the timer."

"Nonsense," said Christopher. "My guess is
that you have quite the competitive streak. So
how about it? We'll be partners but prepare
yourself. I take my charades very seriously."

"Very well then. And you're right, I don't
like to lose," Eleanor said, her mouth tilting
upwards in a smile, her hesitation vanishing.

With each round, Eleanor became more engaged, her stern facade melting away in the embrace of companionship. Christopher was an exuberant performer, gesturing wildly, his eyes sparkling. Eleanor laughed openly like a schoolgirl with each silly guess and triumphant point scored.

"An ice-skating Santa?" she gasped between laughs when Christopher mimed a wobbly pirouette, nearly toppling over in his zeal. But as she called out her answer, she noticed a tenseness in the room. Did she say something wrong?

"Close. A reindeer learning to ice skate," Christopher corrected, and the room erupted with laughter, much to Eleanor's relief. She must have imagined it. Maybe she'd had too much mulled wine.

The jovial nature of the entire Kringle family was infectious, and she was grateful for the chance to see a side of life she'd long neglected—one that included the simple pleasure of shared amusement.

The evening grew late. Rosie and Jack donned their coats and bid their goodbyes. Wind howled against the windows, and Eleanor dreaded driving home.

"Let me take you," Christopher offered as if reading her mind. He stood beside her, so much like Santa Claus in his red sweater. "Sadie or Martin can drop your car off in the morning."

"Thank you, that would be lovely," Eleanor accepted.

They stepped outside, and Christopher whistled for his horse-drawn sleigh.

"You're kidding, right? We'll be blown over the side. Surely my car is better than that."

"Nonsense. See the tall sides on this one? This is my foul-weather sleigh. We'll be fine."

Eleanor climbed into the sleigh, surprised that Christopher was right. They were very much protected from the wind. It was as if they were in some kind of bubble.

"That was a delightful evening," Eleanor said as they pulled away from Martin's cabin. "I haven't played games like that in a long time."

"It was fun, wasn't it?" Christopher said, the wind in the trees providing a backdrop to their conversation. "We will have to do it again some-time. I'm not a bad cook myself."

"Is that so?" Eleanor mused, and then a thought struck her. "You know, I have no idea where you live. Until recently, you've barely been in town. Are you in another town close by or a recluse mountain man who has finally decided to spend more time in civilization?"

She'd expected him to laugh. Instead, he tensed slightly. How odd.

"Oh, I'm not too far, but far enough that com-ing into town takes a bit of planning. I live in a location more central to several of my grand-children, all who run one of our toy workshops."

"And they all live in the area?"

"As the crow flies, it's not too bad," Christo-pher said.

Eleanor still had questions, but as they turned the corner into town, she gasped. Her attention now directed toward a town blanketed in dark-ness. "Oh no," she said. "Not the entire town."

"It's not complete darkness," Christopher noted. "I can see sporadic light from some houses."

"Yes, well, most of us have backup generators for such an event, as I'm sure you do too. But what does this mean for the competition? It's in two days." They passed the Kringle toy workshop. All the lights were on. "Looks like your family has a good backup system."

"We do," Christopher said." We are on a separate power grid."

"What's your secret?" Eleanor asked jokingly while checking the weather on her phone app. She sighed. "Please tell me you'll share your secret because it looks like the wind is here for a while." Her head dropped into her hands. "This is a disaster. I knew the weather this time of year was too unpredictable. Even if we use generators, the tents can't withstand the wind. We're going to have to cancel." She swallowed back tears.

Christopher placed a hand on her knee. "I think—"

"Don't say it," Eleanor instructed. "What I don't need right now are platitudes."

"That's not what I was going to say." He stopped the sleigh and turned to her. "I think I can help. We Kringles are a resourceful bunch. We have a few tricks up our sleeves."

"How?" Eleanor asked.

"Trust me," Christopher said.

She stared at him for what felt like minutes. Eleanor could cancel the event or put her trust in a man she'd only known for weeks. That was a heck of a choice. Christopher, for his part, said nothing, simply giving her time to decide, his expression open and sincere.

Eleanor decided to take a leap of faith.

# 16

ELEANOR CONSIDERED HERSELF A morning person, but the harsh ring of the telephone at 7am pierced through Eleanor's brain and her routine. With a huff, she set down her cup of coffee and shuffled to answer it, her slippered feet scraping across the worn hardwood floor.

"Hello?" she answered, her voice clipped with annoyance.

"Eleanor! What on earth is going on? Get down here right away," the mayor's voice burst through the receiver.

"Can't it wait? I'm in the middle of my breakfast," Eleanor began, but the mayor abruptly hung up.

Eleanor glared at the phone, her lips pursed. "This can't be good. Good news always waits for a decent hour."

With a resigned sigh, she hurried to her bedroom, swapping her house dress for a proper outfit and securing her gray hair into its bun. As she grabbed her coat and purse, she couldn't help thinking of all the things that could have gone wrong.

The walk into town was mercifully short, but a range of possibilities, each more outlandish than the last, flashed through Eleanor's mind. With her imagination running wild, she conjured up images from a two-headed moose running wild to a sinkhole that swallowed downtown.

Eleanor's jaw dropped as she rounded the corner to the town square. There, dominating the center of Mistletoe, stood an enormous translucent dome, shimmering like a giant soap bubble. Not only did it encompass the entire area where the dance competition was to be held, but the entire town square sat inside it, including the giant tree at the center.

"What in the world?" Eleanor breathed, her eyes fixed on the impossible structure.

"Over here," Gloria called out. "I don't know how you did it, but it's magnificent. The mayor is already inside. Come on." She grabbed Eleanor's arm, practically dragging her through one of the entrances.

The interior was even more astonishing—a climate-controlled environment protected it from the raging winds, with strings of twinkling lights crisscrossing overhead and a disco ball like a giant moon in the center.

Mayor Evergreen gazed around in awe. "Eleanor, how did you do this?" he asked as Eleanor and Gloria approached him.

Eleanor blinked, momentarily bewildered. "Me? I didn't—" She paused, remembering her conversation with Christopher. "Christopher Kringle, you know, Martin and Jack's grandfather, well, last night he mentioned he had an idea to protect the area from the winds, but I never imagined this."

As Gloria and the mayor chattered on about the dome's features, Eleanor's mind whirled. How could Christopher have possibly arranged this overnight? It defied all logic and reason. It was as if it appeared by magic.

# 17

ELEANOR WISHED SHE COULD sleep in, but already her phone was ringing. Yesterday had been a whirlwind. Aside from fielding questions about the ballroom dancing dome (she had yet to speak to Christopher), she managed a welcome booth at the hotel for the judges and dancers from out of town.

She also checked in with the band, the caterers, the Snowflake Sugar Shop, Caleb, the local TV station, a ballroom dancing YouTube channel, and made sure the banners for the sponsors were ready.

All Eleanor required now was a week off. Instead, she answered the phone.

"El, it's Viv. I'm back from my daughter's, so put me to work."

It was such a relief to hear her friend's voice. "Will do. I actually need your help with assigning partners. As you know, the professional couples are going to stay with their partners, but for everyone else, we are going to assign partners randomly. I don't know if it's a good idea or not, but it's what the committee wanted."

"Sure. Do I need to worry about the food in my fridge? How long was the power out?"

"Only over night."

"Okay good." Vivian paused. "So are you not even going to mention the giant dome?"

"It wasn't me. It was Christopher and Martin's workers, I assume. No one was more surprised than me, but it works, so I'm not complaining."

"Wonderful. See you soon. Oh, and I'll bring my gown so we can leave together."

Hanging up, Eleanor entered her guest room. She gazed at the dress hanging there. Eleanor had scoured the internet for the perfect dress and knew this was the one from the moment she saw it. The fabric, a deep midnight blue, seemed to capture the essence of a star-studded night sky.

She ran her fingers along the bodice, which, made of luxurious stretch velvet, would hug her torso comfortably, providing support and allowing freedom of movement. It featured a sweetheart neckline, tastefully accentuating her decolletage without being overly revealing. Delicate off-the-shoulder sleeves made of sheer mesh added a touch of graceful maturity.

From the waist, the skirt flared out dramatically, perfect for twirls and spins. Layers of chiffon in varying shades of dark blue created depth and movement reminiscent of ocean waves under moonlight.

But the true magic of the dress lay in its embellishments. Silver and crystal beading, meticulously hand-sewn, adorned the bodice and scattered down the skirt like a cascade of stars. They would sparkle brilliantly under the ballroom lights, creating a mesmerizing effect as she moved.

The overall effect was one of timeless sophistication, exactly what she had wanted. So why was she so nervous?

Eleanor picked up a picture of Carl. "Am I making a fool of myself?"

---

Eleanor and Vivian arrived at the dome two hours before the competition began, carrying the large whiteboard listing the dance teams. And while Eleanor knew what the decorating team had in order, nothing prepared her for the interior of the dome. It was as if she and Vivian had stepped into a different world.

The dome's interior had been transformed into a breathtaking night sky. Thousands of twinkling lights mimicked a blanket of stars, while a full moon, an ingenious projection, cast a silvery glow over the entire space. The effect was mesmerizing. It was as if the roof had disappeared altogether, leaving the ball open to the heavens.

In the center of the dome stood the town Christmas tree, its towering presence both grounding and awe-inspiring. But unlike the Thanksgiving decorations it had donned yesterday, the tree was covered with cascading strands of silver mistletoe and delicate, crystalline moon and star ornaments that caught and reflected the artificial moonlight. The overall effect was a shimmering, ethereal vision that bridged the gap between the town's Christmas tradition and the ball's celestial theme.

Surrounding the tree, the town square had been converted into an elegant ballroom. Caleb had laid a smooth, polished surface that gleamed like ice under the faux moonlight. Tables draped in midnight blue linens were artfully arranged around the perimeter, each centerpiece a miniature representation of the grand tree, but sculpted sugar and draped in edible mistletoe and tiny, moon-shaped chocolate ornaments.

Eleanor grabbed Vivian's hand and moved further into the space. They noticed how the light shifted and changed, sometimes bright as if illuminated by a full moon, other times dimming to create the romantic atmosphere of a moonlit garden. The interplay of light and shadow added an element of mystery and allure, creating an ideal setting for a night of dance and, perhaps, romance.

The dome's transformation was so complete, so magical, Eleanor noted that everyone inside it spoke in hushed tones, as if afraid to break the spell of Moonlight over Mistletoe.

# 18

MAYOR EVERGREEN'S VOICE BOOMED through the hall. "Welcome, ladies and gentlemen, to the Magic over Mistletoe Ballroom Dance Competition. It warms my heart to see such a fantastic turnout tonight. I know you're all excited to get started, but first, let's have a hand for Eleanor Frost, the woman behind the magic here tonight."

Eleanor's knees shook so much that she feared she might not reach the small stage. Public speaking had never been her forte because she feared looking foolish. What would the people of Mistletoe think of her in such a fancy dress and how she'd styled her hair into a French twist? Would they laugh? She longed to run.

Vivian squeezed her hand. "Eleanor, go," she whispered. "You can do this."

Eleanor nodded and made her way up to the mayor, focusing on one step at a time. The crowd was cheering for her, cranky old Eleanor Frost. Maybe the dome had transported them to another world, after all.

"Good evening, everyone. I think we're all in for a sensational night," she began with a shaky voice. Then Eleanor spotted Christoper. He winked at her, and somehow that small, innocent gesture filled her with confidence. She corrected her posture as if preparing for a dance, and her voice grew stronger when she spoke. "First of all, I'd like to welcome our esteemed judges..." Eleanor introduced the judges and the professionals and reviewed the rules for the evening. "And remember, everyone is being paired up at random. Looking to my left, you'll find a whiteboard with your name and partner. Vivian Miller and I will head over to hand out your team numbers. Good luck everyone!"

Eleanor joined Vivian, and they made their way over to the table. The lineup was long, but soon, they'd handed out most of the numbers, and the teams were pinning them onto their clothes. Soon, the band played the first song, and the night started with the professional dancers doing a rhumba.

The final contestant to arrive at the table was Christopher.

"Good evening, ladies," Christopher said.

"Let's see who you're paired with tonight," Vivian said, turning to the board. "Well, well, it looks like you're paired with Eleanor." She shrugged. "Huh. What were the chances?"

"Viv, I'm not supposed to compete. I'm here to help run the event."

"Nonsense. Everything is covered. We're good. And so what if you can't compete, you can still dance. Is that okay with you, Christopher?"

"It's more than okay. Shall we?" Christopher held out his hand to Eleanor.

Vivian nudged her, and Eleanor thought, *Oh, why the heck not.*

"You look beautiful, Eleanor. Absolutely stunning," Christopher said, drawing her hand to his mouth and kissing it.

The moment his lips caressed her hand, a flutter of nervous energy danced within her. It was as if a thousand tiny stars burst to life after years of dormancy. "Why thank you. You look very nice yourself," she managed, her voice huskier than normal. The truth was, Christopher looked better than nice. *Much* better.

He wore a rich, deep black, perfectly tailored jacket with satin-faced peaked lapels that gleamed softly in the light. Beneath the jacket was a crisp white dress shirt with a pleated front. The wing-tip collar framed his face nicely, making his rosy cheeks and blue eyes stand out even more. His deep crimson silk bow tie added a festive touch. His trousers, perfectly pressed, had a satin stripe running down the outer seam of each leg. They broke just so over his shiny black dress shoes.

He'd neatly trimmed and styled his beard to complement the formal wear rather than overwhelm it. And, his white hair was smoothed back, perhaps with some pomade for extra polish. But it wasn't merely his clothes. It was the way his smile warmed her heart, the way his eyes drew him into his world, the way the smallest touch made her come alive.

"You need to know, that what you did... the dome... it means the world to me and I don't know how to thank you. Tonight's success meant so much, and you saved it. I think that's the nicest thing anyone has ever done for me. I won't forget this ever. But I do have one question. How did you do it? It defies logic."

Christopher gave her a disarming smile. "I'm so glad tonight worked out, so let's enjoy it and discuss engineering another night. Let's get on that dance floor. I want to dance with the most stunning woman in the room."

Eleanor blushed, then nodded and slipped her hand into his. Together, they headed towards the dance floor. Christopher was right. Questions could wait. The night was all about dancing in the arms of this wonderful man and nothing else.

As the music changed to a waltz, Christopher turned to her, his eyes playful. "Well, Ms. Frost, shall we show them how it's done?"

Eleanor raised an eyebrow, fighting a smile. "I dare say we must, Mr. Kringle."

They stepped onto the dance floor. As soon as they began moving, Eleanor relaxed into his embrace, their bodies moving in perfect synchronicity. As they danced, the last remnants of Eleanor's years of loneliness and bitterness melted away. Christopher's steady presence, his humor, and the way he looked at her like she was the only person in the room further stirred emotions she thought long dead. And oh, how she reveled in it.

As they twirled, Eleanor caught glimpses of other couples. Caleb was dancing with Sarah from the bakery, both laughing as they stumbled through the steps. Principal Smythe danced with Rowin, the grocery store manager, and moved with surprising grace. People were smiling, laughing, and having fun.

She'd done it.

When they finally took a break, Christopher went to find them bottles of water, and Eleanor moved through the crowd, complimenting everyone on their efforts. Filled with such a lightness, she was certain she was floating. And when Christopher caught her eye from across the room, Eleanor realized perhaps it wasn't too late for second chances, in dancing and in love.

⁓⊸◆⊶⁓

Mayor Evergreen beamed as he announced that Moonlight Over Mistletoe had surpassed its fundraising goal. "And now, with the formalities concluded, here are tonight's extraordinary couples," he began. The air in the dome crackled with anticipation as Mayor Evergreen announced the winners.

"Are you sorry we couldn't be included?" Eleanor asked Christopher, over the crowd's applause for the winners.

"Not at all. The fun is in the participation," he said, putting an arm around her waist and leading her to a quiet corner. "My prize was dancing with you."

Eleanor didn't know what to say or how to respond, but she needn't worry. There was no time to talk because Christopher leaned down and pressed his lips gently against hers.

Yes, *there's something to be said for partici-pation*, she thought before wrapping her arms around his neck and drawing him closer.

# 19

CHRISTOPHER HEARD SHELLY'S ARRIVAL, so he carefully poured steaming water into a festive teapot adorned with painted candy canes. The aroma of peppermint wafted through the air.

Christopher loved his kitchen. Children's drawings covered the walls, displaying the work of three generations: his kids, his grandkids, and his great-grandkids. Each mismatched mug meant something personal, a gift for Father's Day or something funny in his Christmas stocking, because yes, even the head Santa partook in that time-honored tradition, not to mention an ever-present plate of cookies on the counter. As he reached for two cups, the floorboards creaked behind him.

"Morning, Dad," Shelly's cheerful voice rang out. "How are you doing today?"

Christopher turned, smiling at the sight of his daughter. "Good morning, sweetheart. I'm fine, thank you. Care for some tea? It's your favorite."

Shelly nodded, leaning against the doorframe. "That sounds lovely. So, how did it go last night? Did you win?"

Christopher's cheeks flushed, and he busied himself with arranging teacups on saucers. "Oh, well, no. As Eleanor organized the event, she couldn't compete, but that didn't stop us from doing our best. Your old man's still got some moves."

"I bet," Shelly said. "But I thought you said the partners were random."

He chuckled. "Eleanor's friend Vivian was in charge of the teams, so I think there might have been a wee bit of matchmaking." He paused, his gaze fixed on the teapot, steam curling lazily from its spout. His hands gripped the edge of the table. "I think I need to tell you something." He turned to face her. "I've developed strong feelings for Eleanor. And I'm not quite sure what to do about it."

The admission hung between them, as weighty to Christopher as the secret of his true identity. Christopher's heart raced, torn between the thrill of new romance and the fear of potential heartbreak. Given who he was, how could he possibly navigate this delicate situation with Eleanor?

Shelly reached out, taking her father's hand and guiding him to the kitchen table. "Come on, Dad. Let's sit and talk about this."

Christopher settled into a chair opposite his daughter, seeming almost small as he hunched forward. His fingers found a teaspoon, twirling it nervously between his thumb and forefinger. "It's been so long since your mother passed," he began, his voice low. "I never thought I'd feel this way again. But Eleanor, she's brought light and energy back into my life."

Shelly nodded encouragingly, her eyes fixed on her father's face.

"When we danced together," Christopher said, a hint of his usual jovial tone creeping back in, "it was like the world faded away." He laughed gently, and then his expression grew serious again. "But I'm scared, Shelly. Scared of getting hurt, of hurting her. And then there's the matter of the family business."

Christopher's voice trembled slightly as he spoke again. "I want to be honest with her, to build something real. But how can I do that when such a big part of my life has to remain hidden? And what if she rejects me once she knows the truth? I took that chance before, and it worked out. Can I be that lucky twice?"

Shelly reached across the table, placing her hand comfortingly over his. "Oh, Dad," she said. "I know it's scary, but you can't let fear hold you back from happiness. You have so much love to give, and Eleanor would be lucky to receive it."

"What about the consequences? The risks?"

"There are always risks in love," Shelly said. "But you've spent your whole life bringing joy to others. Don't you think it's time you allowed yourself some of that joy, too? Follow your heart. It's never led you wrong before."

The kitchen fell silent. His mind whirled with conflicting thoughts, each one vying for dominance. The fun Eleanor brought him. The gravity of his secret. The fear of rejection.

Shelly's voice broke through his reverie. "Dad, listen. I can't tell you what to do. You're the only one who can make this decision. So, trust your instincts. They've guided you through countless Christmases, haven't they?"

Christopher picked up the teapot and poured each a cup. "You're right, sweetheart," he said, his voice rough with emotion. "And I can't thank you enough for your support. It means the world to me." He paused, absently stroking his beard. "I think it's time I made a choice. For better or worse."

Shelly squeezed his hand, offering an encouraging smile. "Whatever you decide, I'm here for you."

Christopher nodded, then turned his gaze to the window. The snowfall had intensified, blanketing the trees outside in a stunning white glow. He stared into the distance, his mind made up but his heart heavy. The magic of

Christmas, the delight he brought to children around the world, the responsibility to his family and their legacy, that was what mattered.

And yet, as he pictured Eleanor's face, he couldn't help but feel a pang of regret for his chosen path.

The secret of Santa Claus would remain just that—a secret.

# 20

My dearest Eleanor,

I'm afraid I must be brief. The demands of my work have grown tremendously, and I find myself unable to give you the time and attention you deserve. It pains me deeply, but I must focus solely on the business for the foreseeable future. A relationship is not something I can pursue at the moment, as much as it grieves me to say it. I hope you can understand. You are an extraordinary woman, and I wish the circumstances were different.

Regretfully yours,
Christopher


The letter slipped from Eleanor's numb fingers, fluttering to the floor. She stared at it blankly, unable to comprehend the words that had shattered her world. Hot tears pricked her eyes.

"He can't be serious." Eleanor's voice waivered as she snatched up her phone, fingers flying as she typed out a message.

I don't understand. Can we please talk?

She hit send and gripped the phone tightly, pacing back and forth as she waited for his reply. Minutes ticked by, each one an eternity. She checked the screen constantly, willing the "Read" receipt to appear under her message. But there was only silence. Deafening, soul-crushing silence.

Eleanor sank onto the couch, allowing her tears to flow. She had let herself believe. Let herself hope that maybe, just maybe, she could find love and happiness again after losing Carl. But those hopes had been dashed, leaving her alone and broken.

She squeezed her eyes shut, stopping the tears. "I should have known better," Eleanor choked out. "I'm a foolish old woman."

She remained still as a pin on the couch for a very long time. The pain of Christopher's rejection cut deep, more so than she would have thought. She had truly fallen for the man.

With trembling hands, Eleanor reached for the framed picture of Carl on the side table. She traced his beloved features with her fingertip.

"Oh, Carl, I've been so lost without you," Eleanor confessed. "I've been lonely and sad for all these years, but recently I've tried to find happiness again. I put myself out there and now I am heartbroken and left looking like the town fool."

Carl continued staring at her, and she remembered his warm eyes and how they lit up whenever he saw her. He was a wonderful man who loved her with all his heart, and if he'd never taken her for a fool, why should she? Or, for that matter, the people of Mistletoe?

Eleanor had opened up, letting others into her carefully guarded heart. And yes, she had gotten hurt, but she'd gain so much more. She'd gained friends and community. No, she wasn't a fool at all.

Eleanor Frost was brave.

Brushing Carl's photo with a gentle kiss, Eleanor set it back on the table, her fingertips lingering on its edge. It was time to shower and get on with her day. The world didn't stop for a broken heart.

Her heartache would be a constant companion for the foreseeable future, she knew. A kaleidoscope of emotions would no doubt color her days. Yet, despite her weariness, Eleanor realized she harbored no regrets. Joy had finally found its way back into her life, and she refused to revert to her former, miserable self. Christopher had played a role in her newfound happiness, true. But while she could live without him, she refused to live without joy ever again.

Squaring her shoulders, Eleanor grabbed her purse and headed out into the crisp December air. Yesterday, a large team, including herself and Vivian, had removed the decorations and furniture from the dome. And apparently, the dome had disappeared overnight, as mysteriously as it had been erected, for as she turned into the town square, she could see it was gone.

Now that it was December, the town, which always had Christmas decorations up, was in full Christmas mode, and tourists packed the streets. But the twinkling lights and festive garlands adorning the storefronts did little to lift her spirits as she made her way to the Snowflake Sugar Shop.

The bell above the door jingled as Eleanor entered, the rich scent of chocolate and spices enveloping her. She barely noticed the other customers browsing the shelves, her mind consumed with thoughts of Christopher, trying as she might to focus on the task at hand.

"Welcome to the Snowflake Sugar Shop," a familiar voice chirped. "What can I get for you today?"

Eleanor's head snapped up, her eyes widening as they met Nora's. The teenager stood behind the counter, an apron tied around her waist and a Santa hat perched jauntily on her head as if it belonged there.

"Oh, hello, Nora," Eleanor said, trying to muster a smile. "I didn't expect to see you here. Don't you have school?"

"Not today. We got a bonus day off. I can't remember why. Not that it matters. I'm just happy not to be there. Although I didn't realize I'd be put to work," Nora explained. Her brow furrowed as she took in Eleanor's red-rimmed eyes and slumped posture. "Are you okay, Ms. Frost? You seem upset."

Eleanor waved a dismissive hand. "It's nothing, dear. I'm here to place an order for some Christmas gifts."

But apparently, she couldn't fool Nora. The girl came to Eleanor, resting a hand on her arm.

"This has something to do with Great-grandpa, doesn't it?" she asked softly. "I can always tell when it's a matter of the heart."

Regardless of her resolve, Eleanor's composure crumbled at the mention of Christopher. Tears welled in her eyes, spilling down her cheeks.

"He ended things," she choked out. "Said he needed to focus on business."

"And what did you say to that?" Nora asked.

"I asked if we could talk, but he's not replying to my text."

Nora's mouth fell open into an 'O.' "Great-grandpa's ghosting you? I can't believe it."

Without hesitation, Nora pulled Eleanor into a hug, rubbing soothing circles on her back as she cried. A few moments later, Nora pulled back, offering her a tissue. Eleanor accepted it gratefully, dabbing at her eyes and nose.

"Please excuse me, Nora. I'm sorry for falling apart like this," she said, her voice thick with emotion. "I don't know what came over me."

Nora shook her head, a tender smile on her lips. "Don't apologize, Ms. Frost. It's okay to be vulnerable, to let yourself feel. That's what makes us human."

Eleanor studied the young girl. How was someone her age so wise and full of compassion? Nora already knew what had taken Eleanor a lifetime to learn.

"Thank you, Nora," Eleanor said. "Not just for the hug, but for being here, for listening. I needed that."

Nora's smile widened. "That's what friends are for. And you have so many friends here in

Mistletoe who care about you, who want to see you happy."

This confirmed what Eleanor had come to believe. She may have lost a chance at love, but she had gained something equally precious—a sense of belonging, of being part of a community that valued and supported her.

With a final squeeze of Nora's hand, Eleanor straightened her spine, a determined gleam in her eye. She would get through this heartbreak, just as she had gotten through so many challenges before. And she would do it with the love and support of the people she had come to know in this special little town.

# 21

T HE DELICATE CERAMIC ORNAMENT trembled in Eleanor's hands as she placed it on the display table, her sigh barely audible over the cheerful hubbub of the Mistletoe craft market.

"There," Eleanor muttered, adjusting the ornament's position with a critical eye. "That should do it."

Vivian glanced up from arranging a pile of hand-knitted scarves. "El, that's beautiful and so eye-catching. It will definitely draw people over to my booth."

Eleanor's eyes darted around the market, taking in the festive decorations and jolly faces. People were walking around the stalls before the market had officially opened.

"So I talked to my daughter last night," Vivian said. "They will arrive on the twenty-third. I thought, this year, why not have the turkey dinner on Christmas Eve? Then we can all relax on Christmas Day. It's going to be crazy now that her youngest is walking."

"Sounds nice," Eleanor said.

"And I was hoping you'd make the Christmas log. You know I'm not good at desserts. You're welcome to stay the night, too. I can set up a bed in my knitting room."

Eleanor cleared her throat. "Actually, Viv, I've made a decision," she said. "I'm going on a cruise for Christmas this year."

Vivian's eyebrows shot up. "A cruise?"

Eleanor nodded, reaching into her purse and pulling out the brochure brimming with images of sun-drenched decks and tropical ports. It was about as far from Mistletoe, Alaska, as she could get, and that was precisely the point. She was managing her aching heart, but heck, if that didn't warrant a vacation in the sun, nothing did.

Vivian's eyes widened with surprise and curiosity as she flipped through the pages of the brochure. "Well, I'll be. That certainly does look amazing. Tell me more. What ports are you stopping in, and how long will you be gone?"

"It's two weeks long, covering Christmas and New Year's Eve, and we're stopping at multiple ports. I can't remember them all, but I do remember the Virgin Islands, Dominica, and Barbados. But guess what? It's specifically for single, mature adults. No swiping for us. We'll all be together on a boat."

Vivian burst out laughing. "I love you. You're a riot." When Vivian finally stopped laughing, she said, "Seriously though, I hope it brings you some fun, truly. But you're not running away from what happened with Christopher, are you?"

"Running away? Hardly," she scoffed, but there was no real bite to her words. "You won't believe it, but there's a ballroom dancing competition on board." She absentmindedly ran her fingers over a knitted scarf on the table, her mind clearly elsewhere. "There are daily group activities, mixers, outings, formal dinners it will be fun." Eleanor refolded the scarf. "These past couple of months brought back many memories. They've reminded me that life is short. Too short to waste being miserable and bitter." She let out a rueful chuckle. "Lord knows I've perfected that act, haven't I?"

They both laughed, and Vivian wrapped Eleanor in a hug full of love and friendship. Finally, Vivian pulled back, her smile soft. She reached out, placing a hand on Eleanor's arm. "Oh, El," she said, "I'm so happy to hear you say that. You deserve happiness and new experiences. I think this cruise is exactly what you need."

"Well, don't get all mushy on me now," she muttered, but her eyes betrayed her gratitude. "We'd better finish setting up. The market's about to open."

They bustled about, making final adjustments. Eleanor straightened a row of intricately knitted mittens, marveling at Vivian's handiwork. "These are exquisite. They'll sell like hotcakes."

Stepping back, they admired their handiwork. The stall was a wonderland of Vivian's creations—scarves, hats, mittens, and sweaters in festive colors. Eleanor flushed with pride for her friend. "This might not be Santa's workshop, but it definitely has its own charm," she said, sharing a laugh with Vivian.

"Ready?" Vivian asked. "Here come the tourists."

Eleanor nodded, smoothing down her gray bun with one hand. "As I'll ever be," she said, allowing herself a small smile. As the first customers approached, Eleanor thought, *Mistletoe has the best kind of Christmas magic: the people.*

# 22

T HE CHRISTMAS LIGHTS OUTSIDE Christopher's office window did little to brighten his mood. He stared at the pile of reports on his desk, unseeing, his mind a whirlwind of conflicting thoughts. He almost didn't hear Shelly walk in.

"Everything okay?" he asked her.

"I could ask you the same thing."

Christopher attempted a smile, but it felt forced. "Of course, just busy, as always. You know how it is three days before Christmas."

Shelly's eyes narrowed as she took in his furrowed brow and fidgeting hands. "Really, Dad? You can't be honest with me?"

Christopher ran a hand through his beard. After a moment's hesitation, he decided to open up.

"It's Eleanor," he said. "I can't stop thinking about her. In fact, I decided I need to tell her how I feel and why I 'ghosted' her." He put air quotes around 'ghosted.' "Nora's word, not mine." He took a sip of stale coffee. "Nora also informed me that Eleanor left on a cruise. A *singles cruise!* What if I've missed my chance?"

Shelly listened intently, her kind eyes encouraging him to continue. Christopher poured out his worries, his voice growing more animated.

"I care about her so much. The thought that I lost her, that I messed it all up for good... it terrifies me. But I have responsibilities here, to the family, to Christmas itself."

Shelly's lips curved into a smile. "Don't you see? You're using work as a shield to protect your heart."

Christopher blinked, stunned by her words. Was she right? Had he been hiding behind his duties all this time?

"Maybe this is your sign that it's time to retire," Shelly continued. "Enjoy life, pursue a relationship with Eleanor. You deserve happiness too, you know."

As Shelly spoke, hope fluttered in Christopher. Retire? The idea had always terrified him, but now? He pictured himself free from the constant demands of being Santa, spending time with Eleanor, and trying new activities together.

"But what about everything here?" he asked, gesturing around the office.

Shelly reached out and squeezed his hand. "The world won't stop turning if you step back. Let us do this. Our Christmas gift to you. You've given so much. It's time to live for yourself."

Christopher pondered her words. Could he really do it? Take a chance on love, on happiness? As he looked into Shelly's encouraging eyes, a flash of conviction rushed through him. But then the fear came roaring back.

"What about the legacy of Santa Claus? Our family has carried this tradition for generations. I can't help but worry about the impact my retirement would have on everyone."

"That's quite the ego you have," Shelly kindly teased. "But seriously, the Kringle family is strong. It survived long before you and will continue long after all of us. Your children, your grandchildren, and your great-grandchildren will carry on the tradition. It's who we are, too."

As Shelly's words sank in, Christopher inhaled deeply, his chest expanding with newfound resolve. "You're right, Shelly," he said. "It's time. I'm ready to retire and see where this path with Eleanor leads if it's not too late."

Shelly's face lit up. "Oh, Dad, I'm so proud of you. This is a big step, but you won't be alone. Your family will be here to help you every step of the way during this transition."

Christopher felt a surge of gratitude for his daughter's unwavering support. "Thank you. Your wisdom and encouragement mean the world to me."

As he spoke, Christopher's mind began to wander, picturing a new future. He saw himself strolling hand in hand with Eleanor through the streets of Paris, or on a safari in Africa, or anywhere they wanted.

Excitement bubbled up within him, replacing the fear and doubt that had plagued him for so long. "You know," he said, a twinkle in his eye, "I think this might be the start of an amazing new chapter."

Shelly reached out and squeezed his hand. "That's the spirit. Now, how about we see how to get you on that cruise?"

"Yes. Let's do it."

# 23

ELEANOR'S HEART STUTTERED AS the familiar figure of Christopher Kringle materialized among the whirl of ballroom dancers. The grandeur of the cruise ship's dance floor, festooned with twinkling lights and resplendent decorations, paled against the shock that rooted her to the spot. His white beard, a beacon in the sea of revelers, bobbed as he navigated through the crowd towards her.

"May I have this dance?" Christopher asked, extending a hand.

Eleanor blinked. "Christopher Kringle," she uttered, her voice calm and cold. "You've got some nerve showing up here."

He stood patient before her, a nervous smile on his lips. "I know, and I owe you an explanation."

But she held up a hand, refusing to be swayed by his contrite disposition. "You can't just waltz back into my life. Your behavior was both immature and hurtful." Eleanor stood her ground, hoping she succeeded in hiding the whirlwind of emotions that danced through her heart.

"I know. It is inexcusable, but please let me explain. A moment of your time is all I ask."

Eleanor hesitated, studying the lines around his eyes, the dark rings. His expression hopeful and apologetic. If she'd learned anything in all her years, it was that humans had an infinite capacity for making mistakes. Christopher had made a mistake. If she turned away now, deaf to his words, would she be committing one of her own?

If this led to nothing but closure and understanding as to why he disappeared, then that would be enough. If it opened the possibility for more? Well, who knew.

"Fine. Let's talk."

Watching the relief wash over him, Eleanor allowed him to guide her away from the cacophony of music and chattering guests, emerging onto the deck where they were alone save for the rhythmic lapping of waves against the ship's hull. The moon draped its silver glow over the water, casting a spell over the night, and the stars seemed to twinkle in complicity with Christopher's unexpected arrival.

Eleanor shook her head. It wasn't fair that the setting was so romantic.

Christopher took her hand, his touch firm but she could sense a slight tremor. *He's nervous,* she thought.

"I've behaved very badly, and I'm sorry. My feelings for you were growing strong, and, well, I panicked. I used work as an excuse to keep my distance," he said. "I was afraid of taking a chance, of getting hurt. The closer people get, the more there is to lose." His voice held an undertone of vulnerability that tugged at something deep within her. "And I'm more than sorry for avoiding you. I acted like a teenager, but that's because I feel like one when I'm around you. It wasn't my finest moment."

"Go on," she prompted.

Christopher hesitated as if weighing each word before it passed his lips. "My work... it's not the kind you retire from easily," he said, a wistful note threading through his admittance. "There's a reason why I'm always so busy during the holiday season. It's because I'm hiding a big secret."

Eleanor's heart dropped. How often did secrets—*big secrets*—turn out to be good?

"I think we better go sit down," Christopher said, motioning to some deck chairs.

"No. I would like to know now," Eleanor insisted. "I'm not moving until you tell me."

Christopher nodded. "Magic, Eleanor. Do you believe in magic?"

"Magic?" Eleanor scoffed, folding her arms defensively. "Don't be ridiculous, Christopher. Magic is for children's tales." She felt a fortress forming around her heart, protecting her from the ridiculousness of this man. How had she been so wrong about him? "Now, if you'll excuse me, I wish to return to the dance."

"Eleanor, please, wait. Let me prove it to you."

She turned to walk away, but suddenly it was snowing. Snowflakes—impossibly present in the Caribbean—fluttered down, melting as they touched her skin. Maybe it wasn't snow. Maybe it was ash from a fire... or... or something, except it was cold on her skin.

"What is this?" she asked. "Some kind of elaborate joke?"

"It's magic. Santa magic."

Eleanor turned back towards him. Her eyes narrowed, the gears of her mind grinding against the absurdity of Christopher's claim. She poked him in the ribs. "What are you saying, that you're Santa Claus? That Santa's real? You're delusional, believing that you've become the fictional character of your name. Christopher Kringle. Goodness. What were your parents thinking? I'd almost feel sorry for you if this wasn't so hurtful. Why are you doing this to me?"

"Eleanor, please. I know this is a lot to digest but think about it. Really think with an open mind. How do you think it's snowing right now? How do you think I created that dome over the town square or found that beautiful spot in the woods for dancing? How do you think I show up in Mistletoe all the time in a sleigh when I don't live there?" He paused briefly and wiped his hand over his face. "What about Martin's toy factory? How does he always have the supplies he needs? Deliveries are infrequent. Where does he sell them?"

Eleanor decided she needed to sit down after all. She walked over to a deck chair and rested her head in her hands. She had wondered about all the things he'd mentioned. Some certainly defied logic. But no, magic couldn't be real.

Could it?

She turned her face towards Christopher, who now sat across from her. "This can't be real," she said to him, her voice barely audible.

Christopher simply smiled. "I know how it sounds, but if you could allow yourself to believe."

"If you're Santa Claus, what are you doing on a cruise on Christmas Eve? Shouldn't this be your big night?"

"That's where the truth differs from the legend. You see, I'm not the only one. It's a family business," he said simply. "And I've retired."

Eleanor said nothing, instead rubbing her temples.

"There are many of us. Think of it as a business. I am the CEO. My two children, Adam and Shelly, are the VPs, and 8 of my grandkids are regional managers, spread out worldwide. We carry on the tradition, spreading joy and magic across the world." His white beard shimmered in the moonlight, lending him an otherworldly aura.

"No. This isn't real," she said. "Maybe I'm having a stroke."

"You're not having a stroke," Christopher insisted. Before she could protest further, the air around them began to shift. The night sky sparkled with glimmering lights that danced like fireflies. It was as if the stars themselves were surrounding them. Then, in a swoosh, they formed a heart in the sky before turning into fireworks.

It was the most beautiful thing she'd ever seen. Could she allow herself to awaken to the possibility of the impossible?

"Look around you, Eleanor," Christopher urged. "This is Santa magic. Everyone in my family shares this gift."

Eleanor gaped at the spectacle, her breath catching. The lights wove intricate patterns in the sky, and the snowflakes, which hadn't stopped falling either, hummed with a melody that resonated with the deepest parts of her soul.

"And you used your magic to join the cruise?" she questioned. "Or have you been here this entire time?"

"Yes. Magic. I was at home and realized I had made a big mistake by not telling you. Obviously, it's a secret that can't be shared easily. But after a long discussion with my daughter, I realized I was using work and my secret to push you away because I was afraid of getting hurt. Once I realized that, I had to see you. Shelly and I planned how I could board the ship," Christopher revealed, his eyes alight with mischief. "We don't need traditional means of travel; we have our own ways. Booking a room proved more challenging."

Despite herself, Eleanor laughed. Her gaze flitted between the magical display and the man who claimed to be the source of it all. Her rational mind warred with the evidence before her eyes—the undeniable magic that seemed intent on unraveling her disbelief.

"Tell me you can feel it, Eleanor," Christopher implored, reaching for her hand. "The magic is real. As are my feelings for you."

Her hand in his felt like a missing puzzle piece falling into place. The sharp edges of her doubt softened as she watched the lights dance around them, a spectacle of wonder that defied all logic.

"I want to believe you," she whispered.

Christopher's grip on her hand tightened reassuringly. "I've been alone for a long time, Eleanor," he said, his voice laced with a vulnerability that echoed her own. "But when I met you, something changed. I may have Santa magic, but it's nothing compared to what I feel when I'm with you."

Eleanor's chest constricted with a surge of emotion. Was it possible? "I'm trying, but I don't understand how this can be," she confessed.

"Sometimes, not understanding is part of the magic," he replied, his thumb caressing the back of her hand. "And sometimes, taking a leap of faith can lead to the most extraordinary places."

She'd trusted him when he said he could help with Moonlight Over Mistletoe, and he'd come through.

A tear escaped Eleanor's eye. It wasn't sadness that prompted the tear but a burgeoning sense of wonderment. Under the Caribbean moonlight, surrounded by the impossible snowflakes, Eleanor took that leap of faith.

"Christopher," she began, her voice steadier, "I believe you."

With those words, a radiant smile broke across Christopher's face, one that held the promise of new beginnings. He leaned in closer, his breath mingling with hers, and as their lips met, a passion that had been dormant within Eleanor ignited. The kiss was more than a mere touch of lips; it was the fusion of two souls yearning for connection, each kiss a spark flying into the night.

They pulled apart slowly, the intensity of their emotions leaving them breathless. There, arm in arm under the celestial glow, Eleanor permitted herself to indulge in the feeling of being utterly and irrevocably cherished. The magic of the moment—not Santa magic—enveloped them.

"Let's stay like this for a while," Christopher murmured, his voice a comforting baritone against the rhythm of the waves.

"Christmas under the moonlight?" Eleanor asked.

"Under the moonlight with you," he affirmed, and they stood, two hearts intertwined, basking in the ethereal light that promised a future of hope, love, and a touch of magic.

# About Janet Koops

Janet Koops is a Canadian living in Colorado. A former librarian, Janet is a happily married empty-nester who writes full-time from her home just east of the Rocky Mountains. When she is not writing, she can typically be found hiking with her Alaskan Husky or working on a DIY reno project. Janet is a hopeless romantic who loves writing about complex women, their emotional journeys, and the healing power of love.

**For a complete list of Janet's books, please visit https://janetkoops.com.**

# Connect with Janet

www.janetkoops.com
email: janet@janetkoops.com

Goodreads: janetkoops
BookBub: @janetkoops1
Instagram: @janetkoops
TikTok: @authorjanetkoops